MY DARLIN' QUARANTINE

Intimate Connections Created in Chaos

BY ELIZABETH STEWART

MY DARLIN'
Quarantine

Intimate Connections
Created in Chaos

ELIZABETH
STEWART

My Darlin' Quarantine: Intimate Connections Created in Chaos

Author Services by David Ivester
Literary Publicist & Marketing Specialist, Author Guide
www.author-guide.com

Publishing Services by Pedernales Publishing, LLC
www.pedernalespublishing.com

Editing Services by Erin Lenhert
Book interior and cover design: Jana Rade, jrade@impactstudioonline.com
Interior illustrations by Christine Brallier, www.christinebrallier.com
Author photo by Santi Visalli

Creative Management and Photography by John Flandrick, www.flandrickahousephotography.com

Library of Congress Control Number: 2020911081

ISBN 978-0-9981025-5-9 Paperback Edition
ISBN 978-0-9981025-6-6 Digital Edition

Printed in the United States of America

This book is dedicated to my mother, Elinor G. Seifried, 91, who focused my thoughts in this difficult time, and together we worked through adversity.

6

"Round and round and around we go, where the world's headed nobody knows.
Great googa mooga, can't you hear me talkin' to you, just a
Ball of Confusion that's what the world is today. (Yeah, yeah.)"

From "Ball of Confusion (That's What the World is Today)"
by Norman Whitfield and Barrett Strong of The Temptations, 1970

"We mounted up, he first and I the second
"Till I beheld through a round aperture
Some of the beauteous things that Heaven doth bear:
Thence we came forth and re-beheld the stars."

The Divine Comedy, Inferno, Canto XXXIV, by Dante Alighieri, 1314
Translated by Henry Wadsworth Longfellow, 1867

"If you're confused that means you're about to learn something."

Zen Mind, Beginner's Mind, by Shunryū Suzuki, 1970

Table of Contents

BOOK III: THE BIG REVEAL: THE GIFT OF QUARANTINE

Creativity, Companionship, Constriction, and Comedy

The Key to Imagination

This book is a fantasy based on an all too real situation, a quarantine in the face of a pandemic. All of us are now familiar with the tensions and possibilities inherent in the experience of quarantine, having gone through our own. Many of us, I wager, longed to journey through the chaos to reach order again. Perhaps many of us reacted to and thought about those people who traveled through quarantine with us. In the spring of 2020, I had to laugh at life's new absurdities, and I imagined "absurd" one leap beyond our present reality. You are reading that leap!

The quarantine I write about in this book is not endured with loved ones, family, or close friends, but with complete strangers. This offers the characters new ways to act, opening new avenues of self-discovery because they are all outside of their normal spheres of life. Entering lockdown, five groups of strangers have no expectations of each other, and they look beyond themselves. Unfamiliar with their companions, there are no definitions, no previous script, no history of stories told in relationship to others. This is freeing; the characters gradually discover that what they thought they needed wasn't really necessary, and the stories they had previously told themselves were not true.

Five humorous vignettes show that without the complexities offered by chaos, there's little room for change. A re-ordering of oneself and one's priorities is found only through creatively dealing with change. Through my own quarantine, I discovered that change came in the shape of other people, even when I thought I was most alone. And creativity came through necessity. That is something to smile about.

The space we call quarantine is an example of a liminal space in life that we must endure, a limbo neither negative nor positive. Chaos is simply a very complicated space, amusing in its absurdities. This book aims to make you laugh through stories I have imagined about a few ordinary people facing an opportunity to become someone different. Challenges are overcome, creatively and delightfully, in that time of contraction of space that defines quarantine.

These comedic stories explore the possibility that a time of quarantine may be a precious time (for all its frightening "what ifs") because it offers a chance to re-frame creative thinking. Strangers mix-up their mutually impenetrable spheres, and these strange people help each other through chaos. Through these absurd lighthearted comedies, you'll discover that constriction becomes the friend of creativity. Restriction causes expansion for these characters, and it did for me too.

This book was written during the worst days of the COVID-19 pandemic, when four family members tested positive for the virus. I asked myself "What if?" instead of "Why?" When the people in this book ask "What if," the creative process opens up for them too. When time and space are compressed, as in quarantine, the massive power of imagination opens up.

And so, I began to think of settings. I chose five places where I have always felt uncomfortable: a seedy dive bar, a mirrored beauty salon, a car dealership, a dentist's office, and a lawyer's conference room. What if the characters, visiting those places, were told by the Powers That Be that they must stay right there, in place, for 42 days? Following the path of these five short stories, I hope you will find that in the face of an uncomfortable situation, people can and do find unexpected, fruitful companionship. Strange bedfellows help us to discover what makes us whole.

At the heart of the stories are some basic questions: What does creativity look like in chaos? How does humor, imagination, and companionship open the door of that alienation called quarantine? If quarantine is a state of suspended alienation, a handful of delightfully flawed people (aren't we all?) find the space to gather up imagination. The characters invent, make, write, and fall in love, while living through chaos, and they create new bonds and a new order.

If the world as you know it were about to end, would you be doing anything special? For 42 days, the world completely changes for these characters. Each is faced with a past life, and brings that life into quarantine. What makes the quarantine a challenge, on the surface of it, is other people. In the end, the challenge is how to change themselves. What these characters bring out of their bizarre time of quarantine is, in the end, self-discovery, a realization of who they are, what is important for them in the future, why it is fun to laugh at past mistakes, and why it is important to use imagination when the world gets small. Creative imagination gets the people in this book to a bigger world. Once creative imaginations are fired, inspiration leads to discoveries that lighten up lives, both while in quarantine and after.

And so, the characters are left to rely on their own imaginations, which, when activated, have a miraculous way of creating a wake, and the others are pulled along in that wake. Invention and creativity are the tools utilized by the characters to control a situation that they cannot control, to channel positive energy, to get through, and then out of quarantine. The nature of invention and creativity is that one's imagination is in control. Voila! Lockdown becomes a strange place where creative seeds are sown. Creativity gets us out of almost everything, including out of ourselves, even in a serious situation. In the characterization of the presumed carriers of a disease, I am not making light of the seriousness of our future, but I am asking the characters, "Would you like to re-create a future? What will you do?" And then I watch what happens.

The answer is that the characters get busy and create something. They have nothing to lose, because to create a new friend, create art, or re-invent a plan is to say that during a time of suspended disorientation, they can orientate themselves to a new future. They find humor in small measure (and I make fun of them), which is a profound consolation, and I think they will make you laugh too. Any obvious resemblance to anyone in particular is definitely intended.

Thus, in these stories, five outwardly imposed conditions of constriction create an openness to new ideas, and new creative ways to act offered by strange people. Five ridiculous situations of lockdown create a quirky climate of cooperation and collaboration. Humor in chaos lightens things up, opening channels to act upon the biggest question of all: "What do I need from life?" You will see in these pages that life itself provides the delightfully crazy answers to that question.

Elizabeth Stewart, Ph.D.
Santa Barbara, CA
Quarantine Spring 2020

J. Edgar Kirby, Deputy Director
Department of Health and Human Services
Special Health Squad Investigator General's Office
400 East Kentucky Ave, Unit 2b
United States Government, Washington D.C.

August 25, 2020

Enclosed: Your Health Monitor Bracelet number 455999607

Dear American Citizen:

This letter and enclosure delivered to you today will be received by all American citizens. It contains your personal SR-24(a)895 government-issued health Monitor Bracelet, which will monitor your health status. Beginning on August 26, 2020, all citizens eight years and older will be required to wear this bracelet, which has a permanent locking mechanism. When the bracelet is affixed, a sensor will notify us of your compliance. If by August 31, 2020, you have failed to affix this bracelet, trained members of the newly appointed Health Squad Investigation Force will locate you and affix it on your person.

Although the second mutation of the virus is a public health risk, it is not as virulent as the first wave; thus, Government Health Experts are predicting that the likelihood of serious cases is slim. However, the projected illness rate cannot be predicted for the second wave. The average number of cases that a carrier of the virus may cause is known as the R0-Factor (pronounced R-naught). There is a group of "supercarrier" Americans who may be infectious for longer than average. Epidemiologists term these people the R-Factotums. We at the Department of Health and Human Services, in connection with the Centers for Disease Control and Prevention (CDC), have determined that the only way to control this second viral wave is to completely shut down any supercarrier

(R-Factotum) immediately within their environment, when certain conditions of his/her health indicate that peak contagion is probable, for a 42-day duration (six weeks).

Your bracelet transmits a constant record of your oxygen intake, heartrate, and other secret information, and will monitor all others around you reciprocally. All data will be delivered within seconds to our Health Squad Privacy-Minded Database. If the health of others in your environment is compromised, you will see various colors of light flash from your bracelet. (Please go to www.color-codes.healthmonitor.us.gov for specific color coding.) A flashing red light on your wrist indicates that you have been identified as a supercarrier (R-Factotum) of the second wave of the virus, at that specific point in time. Fifteen hundred individuals in the U.S. are projected to be supercarriers (R-Factotums). Although you may not experience any symptoms, we are able to determine the status of the projected 1,500 R-Factotums through our monitoring.

If you see the red flashing light, you will be immediately quarantined wherever you are, with whomever is within 10 yards of you. Within two minutes of the onset of the red light, Government Health Squad Investigation Officers will foam seal your location for 42 days. You, and everyone around you, will be locked down where you are. Windows and doors of your location will be sealed with impassable foam, to be dislodged only after 42 days. Friend to the American people, the German government gifted us the foam engineering technology developed by brilliant German engineers, and used so successfully during Germany's lockdown.

Food, toiletries, and bedding will be delivered daily or weekly directly through one small opening. Yes, we will do laundry. If you have not put a name in your underwear, we will not be responsible. No requests for personal visits (especially from your lawyers), or urgent calls for your favorite electronic devices, for extra phones or chargers, for payments on video game subscriptions, or other pleas will be honored. In short, you will be on your own. Good luck.

More information on geographical locations most susceptible to contagion by the R-Factotums will be released to the news media as we see fit.

If you are discovered to be an R-Factotum, we hope you enjoy the companionship in lockdown.

Instructions for the fastening of the Monitor Bracelet are located on the back of this letter. Please affix it immediately. Or we will find you.

Sincerely,
J. Edgar Kirby
U.S. Government, Deputy Director of Health and Human Services
Special Health Squad Investigator General's Office

Book I

The Lockdown

In Strange Company

Matt   Emilio

20

Chapter I

The Forget-Me-Not Dive Bar

att Early didn't like to drink; he loved to drink. He especially loved drinking in one city dive bar: the Forget-Me-Not on 45th and Figueroa. Not far from his job as a line foreman at a roofing company, the Forget-Me-Not contained a thousand square feet of cheap booze, a kitchen, a 1970s retro bar, a stocked backbar, a back wash station, two restrooms, and a scattering of tables and booths.

It also contained the bartender, Emilio Pugio, about 81 years old, with ample waistline to prove his heritage and a nose that said former alcoholic. He'd been a fixture for 28 years at the Forget-Me-Not, along with the red mood lighting and red vinyl barstools. Emilio didn't much like to see Early's bulky form coming through the front door. He knew Early's whole wardrobe of plaid flannel shirts, various beanies and ball caps, and he was tired of Matt Early. He'd seen him twice an evening for these past eight months. But Early tipped OK.

The problem was that Early didn't talk much. Usually Emilio's clients complained these days about their bosses, their wives, their finances, the damn virus, the cutbacks, the dropped hours, but Early didn't complain. He just drank, paid, tipped, and exited. Early vacated the Forget-Me-Not, for a few hours anyway, around 7 p.m. Later in the evening, there he'd be again at the hand-lettered glass front door. Obviously, he was all dried out. Early's drinking routine played out at least twice an evening. He was one of those silent, but frequent, drinkers.

Men in the bar were all talking, this particular evening, about the State's new regulations around the latest quarantine. During the first wave of the virus, everyone, except very few "essentials," had quarantined at home for three months. During this next "incoming wave," the war against the virus was going to be different, said the State.

The State had done significant social groundwork these past six months. Each citizen had undergone DNA testing in a massive push by the State to gather public health information. All had undergone blood testing and antibody testing, and the statistics were compiled in a State database. Everyone in the State had recently been issued a Health Monitor Bracelet, seen that evening on all the men in the Forget-Me-Not. The guys in the bar talked about the State's new tactics, the new "locked-in-place" Monitor Bracelets, and concerns about privacy. Phrases like "Big Brother" floated across tables, and men checked their newsfeeds about the new laws and regulations coming down the pike.

The State information system reported that evening: "In this coming viral wave, a group of people will be identified as carriers of the virus who are not susceptible to the virus. Fifteen hundred people have, very recently, been found to be future virulent carriers (R-Factotums), but not all will be potent at the same time. Looking at the arc of individual potency, it appears that each R-Factotum will reach the height of contagion on one particular day. Because the second wave of the virus appears, at this early stage, to be milder than the first, R-Factotums may not suffer symptoms. Quarantine will be enacted immediately and in place, however, out of an abundance of caution."

The men at the bar checked their cell phones and newsfeeds to find what the State might do with this new, powerful information. Who were these so-called virulent "R-Factotums"? The feed continued: "Your Monitor Bracelet will be activated if we need to quarantine you. Please be aware the State is applying every scientific tactic known to ensure the safety of the masses." And that was it for official State news: the State newsfeeds went blank.

The older guy down the row of stools, who usually drank straight bourbon, said to the ceiling, or whoever would listen, "The State is not giving us much information, of course. What's that old saying about us mushrooms? Keep us in the dark and feed us shite. That's what we're being shoveled, dontcha think?" The bourbon guy looked wistfully down at his Monitor Bracelet, but no clues as to the State's new plan appeared there.

Matt Early had no interest in the breaking State news, or the rising tide of discussion in the Forget-Me-Not. His face was in his whiskey sour and the music in the bar made it easy not to listen. The guy sitting on the red vinyl stool beside him was trying to show Early his new Monitor Bracelet, a nice shade of dark blue.

"See, buddy, this goes off when I stay in a crowded place too long, or I don't have access to an oxygen feed. We all have to wear these, and now, they say, these damn bracelets are gonna tell us more bad news. If we're one of those poor R-Factotum slobs, this bracelet will flash a red warning light, and then? Who knows what will happen? What color did they send you?" And he looked down at Early's large wrist and odd bracelet.

Early's was green translucent plastic. As the guy gazed at its strange color, it began to flash. The men around Early saw the flashes of red light. Whatever the red flashers meant, they knew it didn't look good. To a man, they threw down their beers and cocktails, emptied glasses, and tossed down their money. Within a minute, only Early was left on a barstool at the Forget-Me-Not.

"Didn't know those darn things flashed red like that." Behind the bar, Emilio, cocked his full, but graying, head of hair at Early. "What's it saying? What the hell's that red light mean? Don't it tell you what it means? Listen to it, chum, it's talking to you!"

Early put the bracelet up to his ear and tried to make out commands, but the bar's music echoed loudly in the deserted room. Emilio yanked the cord abruptly out of the speaker system. The place fell dead quiet.

The dishwasher, Paco, slunk around to the front. The little Haitian waitress and cleaning woman, Jasmine, came out from the back too, along with the massive old cook, Hymen. The four employees of the Forget-Me-Not looked at Early with his green wrist band flashing deadly red.

The Command Voice coming from the tiny speaker spoke loud and clear: "Matt

Early, the wearer of Monitor Bracelet 45097, has been identified as a present potent carrier of the virus, and will be contagious for the next 42 days. Therefore, he will be quarantined for the next six weeks wherever he is located upon receipt of this message. Our GPS system identifies his location as the Forget-Me-Not Bar and Grill at 45th and Figueroa. All people in the building will be quarantined with Mr. Early. At the end of this message you will see a Foam Insulation Rig on Figueroa, sent to seal off the windows and doors of the building, with a small opening left intact for food deliveries. We have identified four people with Mr. Early. Please respond with your compliance on your individual Monitor Bracelets by pressing Comply. Failure to respond with compliance will result in deportation immediately to an undisclosed underground location in Antarctica."

Jasmine, Hymen, Paco, and Emilio glanced down at their Monitor Bracelets, which also started to flash red. They were to be sealed into the Forget-Me-Not with the silent drinker, Matt Early, for six long weeks. Frantic, worried, scared, they looked at Emilio, then they looked at each other. Jasmine broke down and called out to Jesus, then they all looked to the tobacco-fogged front window, where they witnessed the Foam Insulation Rig, and the HAZMAT crew, beginning to haul out the long hoses.

Early smiled sardonically across the bar at Emilio: "One more whiskey sour, paesan, if you please."

Nancy Jean

Elaine

Chapter 2

The Golden Pin-Up Salon

Who slept with whom in 1978, and what she wore to cocktails with him, was always up for discussion in the swiveling beauty chair at the salon on Laurel Street. And the most important question: "During that night of delicious sin, what color was her hair?" When they finished with 1978, the beauty operator progressed her client through history. All the main points, as related to both men and beauty, were usually covered.

At the Golden Pin-Up Salon, hair color changed with men. The beauty operators knew all about the men who had affairs in the small town, and in a more capitalistic way, The Pin's owner, Nancy Jean Hammily, knew real facts and numbers, because sometimes men paid for the color changes. No accounting for men's fantasies; she staked her business on that. She knew exactly what each color change cost each client, and the incoming money (and who paid it) was documented on each client's personal pink three-by-five card.

Nancy Jean was an organized, "bottom-line" type of small-businesswoman, in a small town, on a small side street, but her small shop was big on current trends in decorating, and had indeed changed its décor over the years. Every five years, to be exact, Nancy Jean went to visit her sister in Honolulu, and a paid decorator came in to execute Nancy Jean's design vision.

In 1978, the shop had an au courant, modern psychedelic kind of look. The shag throw rug and the shocking pink of the bonnet hairdryers were toned down by the silk flowers arranged over a white trellis fence repurposed from Nancy Jean's garden, hanging on the far wall. The pink roses spelled out "The Pin." They stayed for five years until they faded to a morose mauve and reeked of Final Net and dust.

On the next remodel, in 1983, Nancy Jean went for yellows and lime greens. The wall behind the trellis was painted True Value's Sunlight Yellow, and the trellis itself was bathed in Gin and Tonic Lime. Little mirrors from Hobby Lobby, hung with green yarn, spelled out "The Pin" on the trellis for the next five years.

Nancy Jean had run out of cheap redesign ideas in 2020, and by then she was getting tired of working, but since she was close to retiring and had a buyer for The Pin on the hook, she'd made it "nice" one last time. Then all businesses like hers were shut down because of the virus, just in time, because the paid decorator had finished her job. At least she had a nice-looking shop to come back to after sheltering in place. In the entryway of the redesigned Pin, straw hats with dried flowers from Nancy Jean's garden lined the wall. She had spent a little extra at Hobby Lobby on real silk ribbons in purples and maroons. New deep red vinyl on the beauty chairs was a big expense. (Of course, her chair was a little nicer than the one Denise rented next to her.) Nancy Jean had also put in a fake wood floor, not so cheap either, although Home Depot had a nice installer-guy for cheap. He was, of course, not tipped.

Elaine D. Jones had been coming to Denise's chair at the Pin for 16 years, and she enjoyed the hats on the entry wall since she had donated one of hers to the 2020 redesign scheme. Elaine was ever so slightly afraid of Nancy Jean, who she knew always had her eyes on her client's pocketbooks. Elaine didn't approve of how Nancy Jean usually tacked on ten percent to your tab for her girls, whether you volunteered a tip on not.

Elaine was hoping that Denise could do something with her roots, because 2020 had been rough, and she had definitely let them go. Gray, silky hairs on her small, precise-looking head mixed with new and surprisingly coarse black hairs, growing unexpectedly where there had once been soft brown. Elaine remembered that a sign of age was hair where you don't expect it. Thank God the most severe social distancing restrictions were over, and she could get back to the Pin.

Elaine was in a bit of a pickle, and not only because of her roots. She was a solid Conservative, and her husband, Bernard, was a left-wing intellectual. They were married after she thought Bernard had "put her in the family way" at Grinnell College way back when. Of course, she was wrong, but at that point she was married to Bernard anyway. She suffered him even today.

One good thing about 2020, Elaine thought, was the way the Republicans had gotten everyone through the crisis, despite opposition by Bernard. She was grateful for the careful gathering of health statistics by the State, and, unlike Bernard, she didn't mind wearing the Bracelet Monitor. She thought of it as a new toy and a badge of obedience to the President.

Nancy Jean saw Elaine come through the door of The Pin, with her mincing little step in sensible small-heeled shoes.

"Hi Elaine. Denise is running a little late today. She had to refile with the Census folks downtown. You know how strict they're getting with counting us these days," Nancy Jean said from behind her tall front desk, which had been painted a brighter shade of purple than was usual outside of the porn industry. (Somehow, thought Elaine, that Adult Shop Purple suited Nancy Jean.)

"Fine with me, Ms. Hammily." Elaine always called other women by their married names. "I am studying the handbook on the Bracelet Monitor. God knows Bernard won't touch the instruction book, so I'll be quite content to wait and read." She primly retrieved the handbook from her small leatherette handbag and began to read.

Nancy Jean was out of her boxes of cheap wine, or she would have offered a glass to Elaine. After the virus, wine had tripled in price, and Nancy Jean would be darned if she was going to spring for wine just to give it away.

"I'm going to make a pot of decaf, Elaine, can I offer you a cup? It's horrible what's been on the newsfeed today. You must have heard that the Government has discovered these R-Factotums that are liable to infect us all over again," said Nancy Jean, flashing Elaine a look at her own orange-toned Bracelet Monitor as she rinsed a chipped coffee mug in the hair-wash sink. "They're saying that we won't know in advance when or where or who is going to be locked down in place with a bunch of poor innocent bystanders. Doesn't seem like democracy to me." Nancy Jean dried the coffee cup with an old black turban towel.

Elaine wasn't sure about democracy, but she was sure that everything was in hand and life would soon be in order again. She was too old to worry about being one of those R-Factotums, and she didn't get out much anyway. Before the crisis, her only weekly excursion was to see Denise Bustamante, her gal at the Pin. "I'm sure, Ms. Hammily, that you and I are too mature and responsible to be anything close to rabid!" Elaine quipped, delicately holding her hand out to take the cup of decaf.

Denise appeared in the bright outdoor sunlight of the small street, as she opened the etched glass door to The Pin with her rear end. She carried a Reynolds Wrapped "made-in-the-pan" chocolate cake.

"I can't believe all the paperwork we've been through in 2020, and we're still filling out forms. That Census redo has us declaring whether we have had the virus or not, and telling on the others at our addresses. Can they do that?"

"My dear, they can do anything they want!" Elaine said. "Elections are for a reason, but after all, it is God who decides who's in charge. And if God wanted statistics and files and forms, which he must have, God is right in showing our leaders his Will."

When Elaine dropped her graying head again to read her Monitor instruction book, Denise winked at Nancy Jean, who didn't trust anyone and naturally thought Elaine's optimism unfounded. Elaine sensed the wink between the other women and looked up, blinking.

Denise caught the empathic drift and parried. "How about a piece of made-in-the- pan to go with your decaf, Elaine? I'm going to mix up your color now, won't be a tick, but why not use the time to try my one-bowl recipe?" Denise didn't offer a piece to Nancy Jean. Nancy Jean had always hated Denise's made-in-the-pan chocolate cake. Nancy Jean didn't much like Denise either. Too airy-fairy, she thought.

Denise slipped behind the plastic beaded curtain that hid the dye room, where boxes of chemical colors lined the shelves. Each gal had a shelf or two because these colors were not cheap. Nancy Jean, unlike more beneficent beauty shop owners, never bought supplies for the gals. The flexible plastic bowls and imitation natural bristle brushes were all privately owned too.

Denise reemerged with strips of foil, two bowls of sharp-smelling product, and two maroon polyester capes, one with kimono sleeves and one that draped over everything on a lady's body. The snaps were getting rusty, but they did the trick. Elaine sat in the uncomfortable, but reassuring, beauty chair and was transformed into a small blob of maroon with a toilet paper collar.

Denise held one comb in her teeth, and one in her right hand, and began to separate Elaine's aging hair into bunches, alternating the bunches with bleach highlight and dye. She dipped her brush into the matte brown chemical dye that she'd been applying to Elaine's hair for 15 years.

Elaine leaned back in the chair, inhaling the curative smell of hair dye. Elaine's back was to the shop entry and Elaine faced her own image in Denise's personally purchased wall mirror with an ornate gold plastic frame. Seated, she couldn't see much below the bottom of the mirror. Being a small, feminine kind of lady, she was lost in the gown's drapery, and was falling into that reverie caused by the smell of toxic hair dye. A little high on the chemicals, Elaine was taking advantage of the fluorescent lighting to study her own face, which did look older, she had to admit. She should have at least refreshed her lipstick before she sat down, she thought.

She became lost in finding the new wrinkles caused by the ordeal of sheltering in place for three months with Bernard as her sole human company. Bernard didn't communicate. He would never say anything like, "Well you sure look nice," even when she tried to make herself presentable for him. Thank the Lord she had her tomcat, Mr. Silkyboy. Without Silkyboy, she would have been a lost soul. No one loved her like Mr. Silkyboy.

Her eyes filled with near-tears of minor self-pity as she looked at the reflection of a face suspiciously similar to her own mother's over at the local nursing home. Life wasn't looking so beautiful, from where she sat. She consoled herself by thinking about the piece of made-in-the-pan she had wrapped and put into her bag for later.

"We cheer ourselves with your pleasures, dear Lord," Elaine whispered out loud. Denise heard pain in Elaine's voice and thought she might have caught a tangle wrong. She stepped back, and spun Elaine around to face her. They both looked down. From beneath those two voluminous gowns of polyester, something was flashing.

Denise's right hand stopped mid-comb, and the other comb, which had been lodged like a pirate's knife in Denise's mouth, fell our entirely, and hit the imitation wood floor, bouncing a few times.

Nancy Jean, from behind the porn-purple front desk, saw the suspicious flashing from beneath Elaine's doubled gowns.

"Get those off of her now, Denise! Let's see what's lighting her up! If it's her Monitor Bracelet, we're screwed. Really and totally screwed. I should have cancelled her when I saw you were late. Both of you are to blame for this! I should have known that this woman would be bad news!"

Red flashes lit up the asbestos-covered white ceiling of The Pin. The Command Voice stated: "Elaine D. Jones, you have been identified as an R-Factotum, and will be locked down at the location you presently occupy: 457 Laurel Street, at a beauty salon called The Golden Pin-Up. We have identified two other women at that location who will be locked in place with you, notably Nancy Jean Hammily and Denise Bustamante."

As Command spoke those two names, Nancy Jean's Monitor Bracelet began to flash red, and so did Denise's. In unison, all three Monitor Bracelets sounded off via Command Voice to the women: "Press the Comply button to signal your compliance. Failure to do so within two minutes will result in the arrival of armed Health Police to take you to an undisclosed underground location in Siberia. The next sound you will hear is the sound of Foam Insulation Rigs sealing off the premises."

With half her head sprouting tin foil, and the other a mess of gray roots, dirty blonde ends, and wiry black curls of indistinct origin, Elaine looked at Nancy Jean, who was cursing with words not often heard in a beauty salon of moderately good reputation.

Nancy Jean spat, "I always hated you! I hated your hair, your name, your bag on your stupid lap, how you always show up five minutes early. I have hated you for years! I hate your little life!"

Nancy Jean had been rendered limp with rage. Denise, on the other hand, was rigid. Her mouth retained the lengthwise shape of the formerly installed rattail comb. One hand held a strip of foil aloft, the other gripped the back of Elaine's chair. One foot remained on the pump bar at the base of the beauty chair. She didn't move a muscle, and her eyes appeared unfocused.

Elaine's tears now had a real reason to fall, and they slipped down her delicately powdered face to the accompaniment of her own little whimpers.

"Oh. Oh, God, why hast thou forsaken me?" she said to the asbestos in the ceiling. "I'm going to miss Mr. Silkyboy terribly!" Tears of loss streaming through pink blush, she brought her Bracelet Monitor up to her mouth, in an attempt to communicate with it. Her hand, with its locked Bracelet Monitor on the wrist, was hard to find under two gowns of polyester maroon.

"Command? Command? Do you read me? Do you copy? Can you give me five minutes to get my cat over here?"

Randolph

Elisa

Dr. R. Edwards, DDS

Chapter 3

Dr. Edwards's Dental Arts Suite

A ccording to social scientists, the type of professional man most likely to cheat when married with children is a Man of the Dental Arts.

Dr. Randolph Edwards, DDS, opened a practice in 1989 in a suburb of Kansas City, Missouri. He was not bad looking, though not classically built. He had expressive brown eyes, curling black hair graying at the temples and not receding much, strong tapering fingers, and, of course, good teeth. He was about six foot two, and because he was formerly a good basketball player in college, he had retained some of the agility of his athlete days. And he looked good in a white lab coat; being tall, dark, and somewhat handsome, white was his color.

He liked the company of his own sex. He was a member of the Kansas City Kiwanis Club before it allowed women to join, and he kind of liked it that way. He had two good male friends, Rev. Angle, a minister in the Methodist Church where he worshipped, and Dr. Leonard Rosenblum, the local orthodontist, who worked down the hall in the Greater Kansas City Dental Arts Building. As a dentist, he was on call for emergencies, and because his social life was hard to schedule, he liked to keep his circle of friends small, local, and mostly, if not completely, male. During the virus Crisis, being part of a tight-knit group of three male friends paid off. As work tapered off because of social distancing, he was still able to talk both God and shop, with Rev. Angle and Dr. Rosenblum, respectively.

He also liked to pass his free time in hobbies thought to be traditionally male. He built an outdoor deck around his family's house, around his mom's house (although he didn't like his mom much, and she complains about the deck to this day), and around his receptionist's house. For his receptionist, who liked very modern lines and modern colors, he designed a deck in silver-toned aged planked driftwood. His receptionist and her husband loved this deck so much that they called it the Good Ship Titanium, and they undertook a nautical theme in the deck chair upholstery to emphasize the point.

In the first round of stay-at-home orders during the Crisis, Dr. Edwards relied on hobbies that he could achieve at home without bothering his wife with too much noise from power tools. One favorite hobby Dr. Edwards pursued was the cleaning of his 15 antique rifles, which he kept in a fruitwood locking rack. The rack hung over the piano in his modest Kansas City split level, which he shared with his wife and three kids. In better times, before the Crisis, the cleaning of these rifles started in late September so they could be perfect by the annual Thanksgiving hunting trip with his wife's brothers in upstate Pennsylvania. But not this year.

Lest we list too many other manly hobbies, suffice to say that Dr. Edwards was not a feminine kind of dentist. Nor did he have feminine traits; at least, he thought his hobbies proved that. He was not the kind of man who would have a woman for a best friend, not even his wife. He hankered after his younger, more beautiful patients, and fantasized about them, but he couldn't flirt the way other dentists have been known to do. He admired his orthodontist friend, Dr. Rosenblum, because he, like Dr. Edwards, was tall, dark, and almost handsome, but unlike Dr. Edwards, he had the gift of gab. He could talk to any woman, even a moderately good-looking one. Dr. Rosenblum seemed to be able to get close to the gals because he was so good at listening to problems. It helped that Dr. Rosenblum was single, even at 45 years old.

Social distancing had relaxed a bit these days, and Dr. Edwards's receptionist, who had been keeping a log of all the non-urgent dental treatments that had been postponed, had compiled a list of patients a mile long for when the stay-at-home order was lifted. Mrs. Folger was a pearl amongst women: a cheerful, roundish, short-haired, efficient sort, who had lost a son in Afghanistan, but who never looked depressed or overtaken by moods. She could be firm, though, when she saw an injustice. She had trained in the Dental Receptionist School of Kansas City, Kansas, across the river from Dr. Edwards's Dental Arts Building. She was well and truly indoctrinated in the belief that all doctors were superior, and all dentists had a both a gift and an art form to practice. She kept the books and the appointments, and also kept up the cheery tone that a Dental Arts office so urgently needs.

Dr. Edwards didn't take much notice of Mrs. Folger in the office (or anywhere else for that matter); he didn't have to. She ran the place so well that he had nothing to complain about. The only complaint Dr. Edwards had those days was that the beige plastic Monitor Bracelet he was sent and ordered to wear by the State was too big for his wrist. Bothersome and cumbersome, it got in the way of the deeper Dental Arts procedures. For example, when Dr. Edwards was faced with dental trismus, a mouth that was too small with clenched teeth, the bracelet could really cause some problems. It could slip right past his tight wristwatch.

A lawsuit over a chipped front tooth flashed in front of Dr. Edwards's eyes as he looked down at his Monitor Bracelet. He would sue the State if that chip ever happened, a countersuit. The State was so intrusive these days. He had heard about those R-Factotum supercarriers of the virus. Being a man of medical science, a dental artist, he thought the science behind the hypothesis was impressive, but the State strategy of "lockdown in place" was excessive. Never mind, he thought, he had been trained on maintaining a clean and germ-free environment as a dental student, so he wasn't worried about being a vector.

On that second week back at full-time dental pursuits, Dr. Edwards had a full slate of appointments. He was anxious to tackle each mouth. All the cleanings and routine procedures were held back to later in the year, and Mrs. Folger had scheduled the more challenging borderline procedures for the dentist beginning that very week. Dr. Edwards liked the challenge of a full week of real applied Dental Arts.

On Monday at 8:30 am, when he came in, Dr. Edwards surveyed the patient and procedure list provided to him by Mrs. Folger on his laptop. Tuesday would be the red-letter day, he thought. A certain patient whom he admired for her beauty was listed in the late morning. He began to plan conversational topics. The patient came from a wealthy family called Morgantown. The family was famous for their horse-breeding, and their studs were the best in Kansas, he had heard.

Tuesday is just a day away, he thought. Since the Crisis, the days either crept by or flew by. He hoped Monday would be one of those fly-by days. It turned out it was a fly-by day, and Dr. Edwards headed home to the split level.

Mrs. Triskel Edwards, or Trisk, was a working woman. She was a bookkeeper at the Nelson-Atkins Museum of Art downtown on Oak Street. She was head of the department and had a few underlings trying to take over her position, but she was not going to let that happen. She didn't smoke pot, she didn't drink; she read books on personal improvement and goal setting. She ran the Edwards household just like Mrs. Folger ran the Edwards Dental Arts office.

Dinner on Monday night was thrifty, nutritious, over fast, and cleaned up thoroughly. The three kids were blessedly quiet, as they were glued to their phones. Dr. Edwards retired to his computer room to watch YouTube videos on barrel rifling reconditioning of antique Winchesters. Since there were six videos offering six opinions on proper technique, he thought he'd be well and truly occupied until time for bed, and Tuesday morning would come fairly quickly thereafter.

Patient one, on Tuesday morning at 8:30, was a Mrs. Hopper, a lady of 70, who had an ongoing case of gingivitis and needed gum scaling. Mrs. Hopper had taken an antibiotic two hours previously and he gave her a big syringe of what we used to call Novocaine at 8:35 a.m. He was slightly annoyed that the usually attentive Mrs. Folger had scheduled such an unsavory procedure first thing Tuesday. He got Mrs. Hopper in the chair—and got her well and truly scraped—exactly one hour after his breakfast of bacon and eggs, with rye toast and tater tots. Trisk had prepared it.

Patient two at 10 a.m., a Dr. Bhuti, was a small man with a small mouth opening, and the damn slippery bracelet did its worst. It did slip, and indeed, Dr. Edwards paused in his protocol procedure to use medical tape to shore up the Bracelet Monitor on his wrist. Would be hell to pay when he had to rip the tape off, he rightly thought, because, as is usual for men who have luscious black curly hair, Dr. Edwards had rather hirsute wrists. However, patient two passed out of the office unchipped and non-litigious.

Then came the impatiently awaited patient three, occupying the receptionist's scheduled slot of the appointment before lunch, which was always a dicey time of day. As anyone who has ever occupied that slot at a Dental Arts office knows, a growling stomach (one needing lunch), either the dentist's or the patient's, is both audible and disruptive, and can be embarrassing.

The last thing Dr. Edwards wanted was to be embarrassed by his fairly well-preserved and healthy 45-year-old stomach and digestive tract. Why? Because this 11:30 a.m. patient was really, really good-looking, and she seemed, from three previous appointments before the Crisis, to be interested in older men with a past; she was rumored to be close to her father and his friends. In Dr. Edwards's imagination, this meant that she wouldn't mind a "friend" with a wife and three kids. Dr. Edwards had been under the impression that certain women like a man with children; he had read it makes them mellow and understanding. Dr. Edwards found himself both intimidated and frightened.

Elisa Morgantown was indeed a knock-out. Even the strip fluorescent lighting above the chair could not harm her perfect 30-year-old complexion, straight white teeth, unplucked and verdant brown brows over equally luscious brown eyes, and aquiline nose. And the chest of this girl! It was akin to what he had heard described as a "rack"—not the kind of rack he had installed for his rifles over the piano, but a soft, curving, art-nouveau shaped sine wave of female buxom-y bliss. It was warm, he imagined, a curve contained in slightly moist and quivering flesh. His imagination was certainly fertile right before lunch! Right then, as he bibbed Ms. Morgantown, leaning over the wonderful bosom, his stomach growled ferociously.

Ms. Morgantown smiled sweetly, and had the good taste not to say anything about the oh-too-human rumbling. Instead she cast her eyes down to a wad of tissue in her hand, held there ready to wipe a sizable amount of Siren Red by MAC off her full and perfect lips. Dr. Edwards noticed, as she did so, the red slash on the tissue, she having just then ardently swiped. Mrs. Folger switched the office Sirius system to the Classic Rock channel, where he heard Mick Jagger crooning the 1965 class c "The Little Red Rooster."

This was going to be a hot hour, he thought. Quietly but commandingly, and in a voice completely male and in charge, he asked Mrs. Folger to turn on the AC.

"Spit please, Ms. Morgantown," he said, as he inserted a wad of cotton roll between her upper lip and her front teeth. He noticed that her labial frenulum was deeply connecting. That realization made his hands sweat inside the nitrile.

Yes, he realized, she was right to consult with him. She had banged her sweet mouth slightly on a trail ride before the Crisis, and that number six tooth, the canine, was slightly chipped. Never before had the ancient name for the long tooth sounded so potent to the youngish doctor; yes, the dog tooth.

"Ms. Morgantown, your canine is perhaps not as sharp as it was before the Crisis. As you mentioned to Mrs. Folger, herein contained in the notes, when your tongue ran over that tooth, you felt a chip on the point." As we all know when we are in the chair, when the dentist engages us in conversation, it is either a mute conversation, and therefore one-sided, or a conversation of a certain bestial nature, consisting only of grunts and gurgles.

The latter was the case then, and Ms. Morgantown gurgled, "Yaaah."

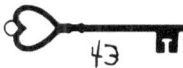

43

Dr. Edwards suddenly loved his job more than he had loved it at 8:30 a.m., and more than he had loved it at 10 a.m. on that Tuesday morning, and that was for certain. He was in love with everything about his job: the drape of the bib over the patient's ample and oft-breathing chest, the feel of her labial frenulum as he inserted the long cotton wad, the clean shine of his dental probe, the supine drape of her long and shapely legs in her jeans over the tapering end of his six-thousand-dollar Dental Arts Ritter chair. Being a dentist, he thought, what a service to humanity! And how wonderful to be alive and of service!

"Ms. Morgantown, we will just take a little off that canine, Mrs. Folger will mix some amalgam, and we will rebuild that dog tooth. By 12:30, you'll never know it was chipped at all," he said firmly and with professional certitude.

Ms. Morgantown said, again, to answer all this professional certitude, "Yaah."

He attached the appropriate drill to the Rotex 782 he took from the side counter. He lost sight of Ms. Morgantown as he turned to tend to his tool. Dr. Edwards turned back and approached the lovely body in the chair. One hand held the Rotex, and one the saliva ejector with its suggestive curved head. Ms. Morgantown, without saying a word, opened wide to receive.

Her eyes glanced down into the deep sleeve of his lab coat. "Argg," she said, alarmed. "Gook ahp yur seeve!"

"What?" said Dr. Edwards.

"Gook ahp yur seeve!" she tried to enunciate yet again. Her eyes were wide and wild.

Past his wristwatch, past the hem of the sleeve of his lab coat, past the button-down sleeve of his pressed dress shirt with its small button, past the very area where the medical tape had fastened to his arm, was his Monitor Bracelet. And it was flashing: red, red, red. Red flashes lit up the artistic and expensive palm tree painting with blue Hawaiian sky on the ceiling of the operatory in that Dental Arts office.

The Command Voice said: "Dr. Randolph Edwards, you have been identified as a supercarrier, and will be locked down at the location we have determined you presently occupy: 6785 Missouri Avenue, inside a private office in the Greater Kansas City Dental Arts Building. We have identified two other women at that location who will be locked in place with you, notably Marian Folger and Elisa Morgantown."

As Command spoke those two names, Mrs. Folger's bracelet, 20 feet away at the faux wood paneled receptionist's desk, began to flash red, and so did Elisa's.

In unison, all three Monitor Bracelets sounded off via Command Voice: "Press the Comply button to signal your compliance. Failure to do so within two minutes will result in the arrival of armed Health Police at the Greater Kansas City Dental Arts Building to take you to an undisclosed underground location in the Cook Islands. The next sound you will hear is the sound of Foam Insulation Rigs sealing off the windows of the premises."

Elisa looked up from her prone position and gagged. Out of her luscious mouth came the cotton roll, all wet, landing with a splat on the six-thousand-dollar Ritter chair. Mrs. Folger came bustling into the operatory carrying a potted plant she had just been watering under the women's room faucet.

Dr. Edwards couldn't believe his luck. He looked up at the Hawaiian palm tree painting on his ceiling, and, with his almost perfect teeth, he smiled, smiled, smiled.

George

Manny

Chapter 4

Sterling BMW of Newport Beach

For 25 years, Manny Nichols had worked a reliable job as a design engineer in Tustin, California. His employment had abruptly ended eight months ago, when he was laid off with a promise of a rehire when the economy picked up again. Manny, a short, single guy in his late fifties, knew he had to tighten his belt and be cautious with his money during that first "shelter-in-place" order in early spring of 2020.

Manny liked his privacy, his small apartment, and good engineering, and the Bracelet Monitor he had to wear went against his grain. He now had little privacy, and the damn bracelet thing was a terrible piece of engineering. He'd been instructed that if he was around an R-Factotum carrier of the virus, the bracelet would flash and instructions would follow. How simplistic, how amateurish, and how inadequate. The State had no sense of design, as proven by their clumsy engineering. Poor engineering design could make him lose his temper.

Manny's greatest love was the design and engineering of a good German car. Every three years since he was forty, he had leased a car he couldn't have afforded to buy. He looked forward to the day the lease was done, and he could think again about the next well-engineered German car he would lease. The Crisis had changed most things in Manny's life, and he hadn't driven his well-designed Beemer much in the last five months. Luckily, his lease was up soon. It's good timing, he thought; at least something was going right for him.

The shelter-in-place order had been lifted in time for him to return his BMW X33 sDrive to Sterling BMW. The lease expiration was a blessing, as his payments were $369 a month, plus his insurance and registration costs, not to mention the cost of the parking garage he had leased to keep the Beemer out of the California sun.

Manny didn't believe in omens, but on a long drive during the "shut down" in April 2020, just to feel the wheel in his hands again, he found himself on a barren LA freeway, and there, he blew out a tire and had a major flat. He realized the Crisis was no time to have a flat on a barren freeway, but with his well-engineered BMW Run-Flats, he made it to the dealership for a new tire. Now his lease was almost up, and maybe driving, as much as he loved it, was a thing of his past, he thought.

Sterling BMW of Newport Beach was a glass-enclosed, Mies-style cubed building on a swanky street. Its modern, slick, and efficient architecture was designed by a trendy German architectural firm. When Manny had leased the BMW in 2017, he had been impressed with the squeak of his shoes on the impeccable German floor, the gleam of the German cars that had been seemingly airlifted onto the showroom floor, and the smell of fresh German coffee in the waiting area, not to mention the elegant German engineering of the expensive BMWs.

His sales agent that day in 2017 had been a Robert Bogdanovite, who was younger than Manny, casually dressed, and with a diamond stud in one earlobe. Manny thought Robert was too young and too fancy to know much about cars, but Manny knew about cars, and he knew what he wanted. Manny accepted his salesman's banter, his stupid pointers, and the leasing terms that were worked out between Robert and his boss, Mr. Sterling, who was apparently hidden away in an office somewhere.

"Now all we have to do is transition to finance, and a great BMW is in your future," Robert said when the lease was ironed out. "The ladies are gonna love you in that X33."

Robert, with a spring in his Adidas and a gleam in his diamond, led him back to finance. Manny didn't care what women would think about his new car. He was a guy that liked good engineering, and nothing else mattered. He bit his tongue, and, feeling his temperature rise, he thought about pulling that diamond earring right out of the salesman's earlobe.

"Transitioning" from the sales floor to finance was a little like moving from the front-row seats at a high-end performing arts complex to the nosebleed seats with the sticky floors. As they walked back to finance that day in 2017, the windowless area of the building, Manny was introduced to George Smithson, the finance guy, who wore a bright orange bow tie that glowed under his thin, once-handsome face.

George's desk was not chrome and glass like the desks on the sales floor; his desk in finance was 1970s brown Formica. A picture of someone who appeared to be his mother was displayed in a cheap Aaron Brothers frame on the desk, and a case of imported Tetley Earl Grey loose-leaf tea was on the floor. Manny took a seat in an old, black, vinyl armless chair, four feet away from the front of George's desk.

Pieces of Formica had fallen off the bottom of George's desk, where the janitor had aggressively cleaned the linoleum floor with a vicious mop for years. The computer on the side was circa 2005, and the printer hailed from the days when printer paper came on a roll with perforations on the sides.

George was efficient, numerate, and thorough. The process went smoothly until George Smithson looked up from his numbers and percentages and tried to sell Manny the Sterling BMW "extras."

"We recommend you purchase our 2017 Mica Seal package, because, you know, in 2020, when you return the Beemer, you could be charged fees for excess wear and tear. This Mica Seal treats the leather on the seats so not even your grandkids can mess up the leather." George sounded like he had been coached to promote Mica Seal, and Manny could tell that he hated the thought of selling anything to anyone.

Manny hoped the grandkid comment was scripted, although it did make him mad, nonetheless. Not only was Manny not going to buy a fifteen-hundred-dollar seat treatment, he was not a grandfather, and in his opinion, he didn't look old enough to be a grandfather! He felt hot under the collar. He couldn't help but hate this skinny, pencil-pushing former accountant in dingy finance.

George, as he tried to sell the extras, was not looking at Manny, but he continued as if he were on auto-pilot: "We also recommend our PermaPaint, our best recommendation for keeping the color of the car exactly as you see it now. The sun is rough on cars here in Southern California. On average, we charge two thousand for severe sun damage on returned leased vehicles, and that makes the PermaPaint a deal at a thousand. It's a quality product, invented right here in Southern California, just for our own California sun." George slid a brochure across the desk, which showed a team of scientists in Japan clustering around a Lexus in a brightly lit lab.

Manny glanced at it and said, "No, I think I'll pass on the paint treatment." Manny was clearly losing his patience. He was getting mad and hot, and he feared he would lose his temper. He was thinking about walking out on this little man in the orange bow tie. "Any idea how much longer I need to be with you? I have other things to do today." Manny was thinking about ripping that bow tie off the skinny neck of this finance guy. But something about George Smithson's regretful and sad face made Manny pause.

Fearing to say or do something he might regret, Manny pulled his credit card from his wallet, and tapped it violently on the desk, making sharp, percussive noises. George was alarmed at the fierce gesture and tone of this client. However, he was more fearful about his job. He couldn't lose this deal. Mr. Sterling would fire him.

In a small voice, George said, "I was trained as a CPA, Mr. Nichols, and not as a salesman. The extras are something I must promote. If Management asks, please tell them I tried." He sounded so pathetic that Manny had to keep quiet.

The 2017 battle at the dealership was finally won that afternoon, years before the Crisis, and Manny happily drove the shiny subtle-brown BMW X33 home to his small place in Tustin. He had driven his well-engineered car to and from work every day until April of 2020, but he hadn't driven it much lately, shocked by the deserted streets of the Crisis. He thought about driving less in the future, as he had acclimated to working at home. Manny, for the first time in his life as a German car lover, was happy that he wouldn't be leasing a new one.

He searched and found the finance guy's card in his lease paperwork and placed a call to George Smithson at Sterling BMW. "Mr. Smithson, this is Manny Nichols. You did my paperwork on a 2017 BMW X3 sDrive. The lease is over in two weeks and I want to make arrangements to drop it off."

George replied as if he was reading from a script: "We're not accepting leases back. If you want to make arrangements to drop off the car, call BMW." And then he hung up.

Manny pulled the phone from his ear and looked at the phone's screen in disbelief. He called Sterling BMW back and again asked for George.

"Mr. Smithson, you hung up on me, damn it. This is Manny Nichols. My 36-month lease is over, and I want to make arrangements to drop of the Beemer now! In two weeks, the lease will expire."

George replied in a small, flat voice, "We are not accepting leases back. If you want to make arrangements, call BMW in Woodcliff Lake, New Jersey."

Manny was incredulous. He was furious. The damn world had changed. Manny was reminded of the change each morning when he woke up and realized he was wearing a Monitor Bracelet. And now a change in leasing and returning a nicely engineered German car at a high-end dealership! Maybe the State had let the high-end dealers off the hook, just like the State's officials didn't have to wear a Monitor. Maybe international corporations did not have to follow through on their promises. Maybe the little guy always gets the shaft, he thought, and getting hotter and more agitated, he called again.

"May I speak to your boss, Mr. Smithson," he shouted into the phone.

"Hold while I transfer you," said George, relieved to transfer the call.

Manny held the phone from his ear and grimaced as he listened to car dealership hold music, and said to himself, "I can handle one song, but if they play me another, I am going to throw this phone off the balcony!" Five songs later, Manny was still on the line. His face was beet red.

"This is Mr. Sterling, how may I help you?" said a deep and confident voice at long last. Manny explained tensely that he wanted to end his lease and bring back the Beemer.

"We are not accepting leased cars back," Mr. Sterling said, "but we are offering lease extensions. We are not offering forgiveness of payments if you do decide to extend the lease, but in cases of hardship, we are offering deferred payments." Manny felt like punching the wall of his apartment.

Manny yelled back, "I just want to drop of the car. I don't want to pay for garaging, insurance, and registration! And the lease is over. Expired! I don't want a lease extension. What are you going to do about it?"

"Will you lease a BMW as your next car?" Mr. Sterling replied.

Manny took the bait: "Of course!" He had no intention of doing so, but understood Mr. Sterling's drift.

"Come in and see George Smithson, and he will talk to you about your options," Mr. Sterling said, "When would you like to come in?"

Manny made an appointment for Friday at 2 p.m.

Bossman Mr. Sterling put down the phone, and immediately marched into George's finance office. George was wearing a bright blue bow tie that was slightly off kilter. When Mr. Sterling entered, George's hand flew up to straighten the tie. His Monitor Bracelet caught on the tie. George was scared stiff.

"Look, Smithson, a client wants to return a leased X33, a guy named Manny Nichols. He's coming in this Friday. Under no circumstances are you to let him return that leased car. It's 2020, and new vehicle sales are down 67% and used sales are down 64%. I would rather fire you than have to deal with a lease return on a 2017 X33. You will be fired if Nichols leaves his car in our lot. No returned leases! Your job is on the line. Talk him into paying monthly for a lease extension. That's the company policy from now on. Am I clear?"

"Mr. Sterling, I'm not a salesman," George said, "I'm a numbers guy. But I'll do it, boss."

Mr. Sterling spoke louder, "Friday at 2 p.m., when Nichols comes in, I am locking this office door from the outside. I will unlock it when you call me and tell me he's extending his lease." He turned on his heel and slammed the finance office door.

Friday at a quarter to two, Manny pulled the BMW X33 into the packed lot of Sterling BMW. No one was in the beautiful showroom. He remembered the way to finance and let himself into George Smithson's office. He was prepared to fight and fight hard. Smithson's office was shabbier than he remembered it, and the framed photo of his mother was gone from the desk. Where there had been a box of English tea in 2017, Manny now saw a cardboard box filled with hand sanitizer. Manny sat down.

Mr. George Smithson, alarmed, saw from the hallway that Manny was seated in his office. He slunk to the far side of his desk and sat in his faded high-backed executive chair.

"Here are the keys, Mr. Smithson," Manny said, "Inspect the car, and let me out of this lease."

George got up his meager nerve and said, "We have no one to inspect the car because we are not accepting lease returns. Your only option is to take a lease extension at the same monthly payment."

Manny took a few steps back, as if getting ready to throw a punch. His color was rising, and George was unable to look him in the face. George wished he had never seen Manny Nichols. His job was on the line, and these days, no one wanted to hire a 56-year-old ex-CPA. He needed this job.

George put on a tone of bravery. "Look Mr. Nichols, you have no choice. This is BMW policy."

Manny stood up. He pointed an aggressive finger at George's chest. "I'm not responsible for this car. I am leaving it here!" With each word, Manny emphasized his anger with a finger jab in George's direction.

George's mouth flew open. Manny's Bracelet Monitor was flashing red, red, red.

The Command Voice emanating from the Monitor said, "Manny Nichols, you have been identified as an R-Factotum, and will be locked down at the location we have determined you presently occupy, which is 896 Coral Drive, Newport Beach, in the finance department of Sterling BMW. We have identified another male at that location who will be locked in place with you, namely George Smithson."

As Command spoke, George Smithson's bracelet, resting on the Formica desk, began to flash red in unison with Manny's. Both men's Monitor Bracelets sounded off, via Command Voice: "Press the Comply button to signal your compliance. Failure to do so within two minutes will result in armed Health Police arriving at Sterling BMW Finance Department to take you to an undisclosed underground location in the Galapagos Islands. The next sound you will hear is the sound of Foam Insulation Rigs sealing off the windows of the finance office premises."

Manny bolted for the door, his shoulder ready to spring the hinge off the frame, but Mr. Sterling had locked it shortly after he saw Manny enter. Manny turned to throw a punch at George Smithson, but George was huddled under his Formica desk, sobbing.

Reedley

Amalie

Carol

Chapter 5

Liederkranz, Campbell, Sheffield, and Spray LLP

Fantasies can happen in any stage of life, but there's a certain kind of sexual fantasy that typifies male menopause, especially when the middle-aged man involved has been living with the same woman through certain segments of time. Namely, when he has lived with her for multiples of seven years. Biological scientists tell us that every seven years, the human body changes all its cells completely. Have you heard of the seven-year itch? Perhaps there's a biological reason for a 50-year-old man fantasizing about a younger, hotter woman; that could be the itch at work. It makes a man want to build himself a new life, or perhaps build a new woman.

Reedley Liederkranz was at this stage of his biological life, and his imagination kept him up at night. Yes, he was sleeping next to his wife of 28 years, Carol Abrams Liederkranz, but she was a good sleeper and didn't hear him tossing and turning. Reedley's Monitor Bracelet caught on his pajamas repeatedly, adding to his discomfort.

Even if Carol had been a light sleeper, she might have missed the turmoil next to her. Every seven years of marriage, the couple had invested in a bigger bed. Twenty-eight years of marriage had earned them the Sleep Number 360 i8 California King Smart Bed, with its two separate mattress panels. The bed, which cost them around five thousand dollars, tracked sleep on its computer. Tracking sleep patterns was about the only thing Carol wanted to do in bed these days, however. Fine with Reedley. He was in bed designing and building his perfect woman.

That's not to say that Reedley didn't love his wife; he thought of her as his equal, a good friend, a real intellectual match. They had met at Harvard where she was studying law and he was in the graduate theology program. Late-night conversations revolved around ethics, morality, and responsibility, as you might have assumed would be topics for a future lawyer and future pastor.

Now Carol was a sought-after trusts and estates lawyer in the city of Washington,

D.C. Since the Crisis of 2020, she had been working especially diligently writing wills, trusts, and medical directives for end of life issues. She had made enough money in her career that she didn't need to rely on Reedley's salary, but that was not always the case. When they were first married, Reedley's income as pastor of the Methodist Church of Arlington, Virginia, had kept them afloat.

But that was 28 years ago, and now Carol was the breadwinner. In fact, Reedley worked for her. Reedley's tenure as a pastor had lasted about seven years. (He had had a misunderstanding with a 17-year-old high school senior in his Christian Youth Outreach.) He changed careers, and, following his wife's sage advice, became a financial consultant to many of Carol's clients.

Reedley relied on Carol for his nicely decorated and well-situated home in Arlington, he relied on her to introduce him to her clients, and he respected her capabilities and talents. Conversation since the Crisis of 2020 was about work. The financial needs of her clients were discussed at home, and the legal frameworks of trusts, along with trustee issues (Carol was trustee for many of her wealthier Washington, D.C., clients) were aired at dinner. Reedley admired the way Carol could both make a meal and discuss the finer shades of legal matters. Yes, Carol was brilliant, accomplished, and a great multi-tasker. Reedley told himself that, after all, he was a lucky man. He lacked for nothing, at least materially speaking. She even picked out his business clothes and shoes.

However, nights upon the Sleep Number bed were long and hot for Reedley, who had a project, a construction project, we might say. He was employed in building the perfect woman for himself, from the top of her head to the bottom of her feet, as he laid in bed with Carol. On some nights, he would change a few features, and rebuild the woman, much like a new car buyer would build a new car on the Mercedes website, perfecting the shape, the model, the color, the extras, and the size of the engine, built from the chassis on up. Just so did Reedley endeavor, each sleepless night, to build his dream mate.

The project was coming along nicely. She was hot, he thought, but not the hottest young woman. Not supermodel hot, but the kind of hot that you notice in a crowd. Not the kind of hot that made a woman self-centered. No, she was obligingly hot: she had long brown hair, and something of a girlishness about her hairstyle—he thought she might wear bangs. Yes, bangs. She had straight serious brows, not arched and inquiring like Carol's, but straight and earnest. Brown eyes, very large, but not dark brown like Carol's. No, a light brown, with gold flecks. He had seen eyes like that once on a high school sophomore at his Annual Young Life Chaperoned Retreat. Brown eyes with the sun inside, a sun that encircles the pupil. Really sexy, he thought, a small imperfection in a young woman's huge, beguiling, innocent, flecked brown eyes.

And then the nose: not a huge nose, but nonetheless a little larger than pug or bobbed. Something that had a bridge, of course, but not too high of a bridge. And not a nose like Carol's, which had a very high bridge and was perfect for her fashionable but businesslike horn-rimmed glasses.

He fondly remembered a perfect nose he had encountered when he and Carol broke up for a few months back at Harvard. He had gone bowling with a girl with such a nose. Afterwards she was eager to kiss him, and more, on the way home. He remembered that her nose was flattish from the bridge, which meant she could bury her whole face in his lap. He thought about that kind of nose and what a girl who had it could do in bed. So, he added a flat-bridged nose to the long brown hair with bangs and straight brows and innocent sun-filled eyes. Good.

The mouth—very important—was kind and delicate, full and pink, and untouched by lipstick (unlike Carol's, which wore Rubinstein's Relentlessly Red). He built in some small, white teeth, with a slight gap in front, and an ever-so-slight overbite. Just to prove that he wasn't after the hottest woman in the world, he added a wispy little blonde downy mustache. It was the kind of down you see only in the July sun ight at the beach, and which is also found on egs and down the centers of flat young stomachs. He remembered the Word of God Beach Party in 1983 and the peach fuzz on the flat stomach of the star of the bikini volleyball play-off. (What was her name again?) Peach fuzz, yes, not the Nair stubble his wife used to sport, oh no.

Long neck, of course, and no jewelry ever, nothing like the double strand of pearls Carol thought a classy touch for days in court. And if his dream girl had to wear jewelry, he thought, a little sterling crucifix might be delicious during wild sex.

Then the breasts: not large, just right, small handfuls he thought they were called, and pink nipples. Small waist. He built her to be about five foot four, not almost six feet tall like Carol. She didn't have to have long legs. Carol's were almost too long and looked kind of horse-like in skirts. He wanted athletic, shorter legs and a firm butt that kind of poked out at a man.

Small feet, very small, and he didn't build her in high shoes. No high heels, no platforms, just dainty feet in a simple pair of worn brown leather boots with chunky heels and zippers on the sides. And she would be a casual dresser, tending to be earthy-crunchy in her bohemian style; kind of farmer's market sexy, with halter tops and big, easy-to-lift peasant skirts and blouses. Yes, not the type for tight jeans, like Carol wore in law school. Easy, flowing clothes that could stay on the bedroom floor all night long.

She was almost "all built" those days, but Reedley always fell asleep before he could build his perfect woman's mind, character, or intellect. Usually after the body was built each night, he could sleep for four hours. He never got around to her mind or the other incidentals.

Morning came and kicked him. Carol was already up, thank God, and making breakfast. She was always dressed before he was and organized for a day at her office, having gathered her papers and laid out her business suit the night before. They had separate dressing rooms and bathrooms.

Reedley pulled off his pajamas, ripping the sleeve on the Monitor Bracelet, and dressed for work. He was going in with Carol to meet a wealthy family who needed his advice on setting up a 529 for their grandson for college. Commissions for those deals weren't bad. He dressed with care in a business suit and fished out a pair of brown Oxfords, a gift from Carol that he hated.

Never mind, he must look the part when talking other people's money, he thought. He could handle one morning of Carol's uncomfortable brown Oxfords. For the kind of money contained in the Funicle family trust, he could have sore feet. He would be pleased to meet Dr. and Mrs. Funicle; Carol said they were bringing their grandson, too.

Reedley wished they were bringing a granddaughter, but heck, she might be just a kid. A guy could only dream, he thought, and, sadly, never touch when they were that young. He tied his tender morning feet into the stiff Oxfords. A metaphor for his life, he thought, those shoes. He wished he was still in bed building his dream.

Carol's office suite at Liederkranz, Campbell, Sheffield, and Spray LLP occupied one whole floor of a brownstone in downtown D.C. It was appointed in 18th-century American style as suited the town. Carol had done a magnificent job of decorating: the office said established and classy. The conference room featured a huge flecked marble table and mahogany Chippendale chairs, with a credenza that held a beautiful espresso maker and a stack of legal pads with Carol's name across the top.

The Funicle family was shown in by the ancient receptionist a few minutes after Carol and Reedley parked Carol's expensive car. The family were installed on the Chippendale chairs around the conference table. Carol introduced Reedley to Dr. and Mrs. Funicle, and a young man of eight, their grandson Robert.

"And Robert, this must be your mother?" said Carol, smiling at a 24-year-old woman seated next to Dr. Funicle.

Oh my God, thought Reedley, the world had stopped. All thoughts left Reedley's head: social distancing, financial advice, business propriety, gracious manners, who he was, and who the tall woman next to him was, or who she had ever been to Reedley. The world ceased to spin. Reedley went weak in the knees.

It was her. She was right there. The exact make and model he had built during many sleepless nights on the Sleep Number mattress right next to Carol's long, soundly sleeping body. She, his dream, was seated before Reedley in Carol's conference room.

Yes, by God, he knew it was her. Brown hair with bangs, straight brows, light brown eyes with gold flecks of sun inside, a flattish nose over full unadorned lips, a gap between her white incisors, a long neck on which hung a silver crucifix, a peasant blouse with an open and inviting neckline, a full draped skirt, and shapely athletic legs in worn, brown zippered boots. He extended his hand to shake hers, in the old style of welcome before the Crisis. All he wanted was to touch his dream's hand. Please, dear God. Let me touch her. Was she real, or the extension of a builder's dream?

Carol smiled at the family around her conference table. "Reedley is so thrilled to meet you all that he forgets we don't shake hands these days. Especially since we have all been instructed to wear these Monitor Bracelets in case we encounter a supercarrier of the virus. Life has changed, hasn't it? But good legal and financial advice will always be needed!" Turning to Robert's attractive but slightly counterculture mother, Carol asked, "What is your name, please?"

The younger, smaller female answered, "Amalie," and smiled shyly, but beguilingly, at Carol.

Reedley was on a planet that had ceased to rotate, and he had lost track of his right arm. It was still extended in an offered handshake. He felt himself walk across the conference room in those constricting Oxfords, and he pulled out the Chippendale chair across from Amalie's with his left hand, which was attached to his movable arm.

Carol looked at her husband in some confusion. "Well, Reedley," she said, a bit annoyed at his stupefaction, "I'll shake your hand!" And she grabbed his extended right hand and shook it hard.

As she did, Reedley's Monitor Bracelet began to flash with three short bursts of blinding red light. Dr. Funicle, Mrs. Funicle, young Robert, and Carol all looked at Reedley's extended arm in horror.

"Jesus H. Christ. He can't be an R-Factotum," said Dr. Funicle, and jumped in obvious agitation to shield his daughter from Reedley's extended right arm and hand.

"Get away from my family!" he said. "You're threatening my daughter with your filthy hand! Get away!"

As he said these words, Dr. Funicle's bracelet began to flash red, as did his wife's, Amalie's, Carol's, and young Robert's, too. The Command Voice emanating from Reedley's Monitor Bracelet said: "Reverend Reedley Liederkranz, you have been identified as an R-Factotum, and will be locked down at the location we have determined you presently occupy, which is 346 Stratton Ferry Road, Washington, D.C., on the second floor of Liederkranz, Campbell, Sheffield, and Spray LLP. We have identified five other individuals at that location who will be locked in place with you, namely, your wife, Carol Abrams Liederkranz, Dr. Leonard Funicle, Mrs. Mary Funicle, Amalie Mercedes Funicle, and her son, Robert Ford Funicle."

From all wrists around the marble conference table, Monitor Bracelets sounded off, via the Command Voice: "Push the Comply button to signal your compliance. Failure to do so within two minutes will result in armed Health Police arriving at Liederkranz, Campbell, Sheffield, and Spray LLP to take you to an undisclosed location underground in Lagos, Nigeria. The next sound you will hear is the sound of Foam Insulation Rigs sealing off the windows of the second floor of Liederkranz, Campbell, Sheffield, and Spray LLP."

Reedley dropped his extended arm, upon which the Monitor Bracelet was still flashing its red, pulsating warning. He stood up from his Chippendale chair, across from Amalie's. Standing very still upon his Oxford shod feet, and gazing at Amalie Mercedes Funicle, he urinated down one pant leg. He completely flooded one brown shoe, the left mate of that painful and metaphoric pair of Oxfords. Reedley did not feel it at all.

Book II

The Creative Inspiration

The Art of Being Together Alone

Chapter 6

An Inspirational Bar Fight

Looking up at the Forget-Me-Not's red ambient mood lights and the red vinyl bar stools, Matt Early checked his Monitor Bracelet. No more red flashing warning lights. How embarrassing that had been. He tucked the wrist with the monitor into his Carhartt jacket.

If he had to be holed up, his favorite dive bar was not so terrible, he thought to himself, satisfied. He could drink six weeks away, no problem; he just didn't want to talk to anyone. He ordered his fourth whiskey sour from Emilio, who could hardly believe the satisfaction on Matt's face.

Matt's Monitor Bracelet had flashed one hour before. He should be apologizing, making amends. But Matt didn't want to do anything but drink. He didn't want to think. Shy, withdrawn, he couldn't face adversity. He ran from it, especially if there were other people involved. People were the main cause of pain, he thought, and they always caused problems.

Emilio feared what would come of six weeks of Matt and his drinking and his damned alienation. He was not pleased that Matt was getting hammered without so much as an acknowledgement of the quarantine—a 42-day marathon—that Matt had brought down upon Emilio's head. Not only Emilio, but also his staff, would be locked down with this sad drunk. One hour into a 42-day quarantine, Emilio didn't know what to think, what to do, or how to prepare, and Matt was a lump on his barstool.

The Budweiser clock on the back bar read 11 p.m. The State's foam rig trucks had sealed all doors and windows but one. It was to be used for food delivery, as succinctly stated in a State official letter dropped through the window's slot.

The dishwasher, Paco, was in the back kitchen speaking frantically with his girlfriends over his cell, as he had been for the past hour. He was letting them know that he was very angry. Wild curses in Spanish reached Emilio's hearing now and again. Paco, who loved his motorcycle and his many girlfriends, would surely be impacted by this forced confinement. Enough crying women had made their dismay known in just that one hour—you could hear wailing over the phone—that Emilio knew he'd have a frustrated Lothario on his hands within two days.

And little Jasmine, the waitress and cleaner, who had no one to call, was miserable. She was installed in a red vinyl booth with her head on the table and her hands over her dreads. Her family was back in Haiti, and she couldn't get them on the phone. She needed some reassurance that she would be okay, more assurance than her crucifix could give her.

Hymen, the cook, had swung into action and was cooking burgers and fries for the five of them.

Matt was focused on his drink, not speaking, and showing no emotion at all.

If someone had to be in command of the Forget-Me-Not and its staff for a six-week quarantine, Emilio was a good choice. Emilio was no stranger to deprivation. He had been a schoolboy during World War II and had seen his family home in Sicily destroyed and his parents captured. He and his brothers escaped to a nearby abandoned farm and locked themselves inside for three weeks. Emilio had only scraps from the garden to feed himself and his two brothers. He knew what privation felt like, and he knew that every difficult situation had an ending, whether the ending was happy or not. But the lump of a drunk at his bar seemed to think that this was just another night.

It wasn't. It was the start of a long journey.

Emilio faced Matt, remembering his childhood and how he had fought to stay alive. He said, "Buddy, you can't just drink for six weeks. You gotta sleep; you gotta eat. It's late. I have a few thoughts. There's six long banquettes in the front booths by the window. I want you to pick one and make that your bedroom. There are stacks of clean towels used for the kitchen. Take a few for bedding. And you have your jacket for a blanket. You gotta look after yourself. Hymen is cooking, and after we eat, let's get some sleep. Tomorrow we'll talk. This is my bar, and I'm in charge now."

Matt simply pointed to his glass and signaled for a refill. Emilio shook his head, but he fixed Matt another cocktail.

The next morning was tough. Matt was beyond talking. Thank God no one was up yet. Matt's banquette at the front of the bar was closest to the window, and the gray morning sun hit him in the face. His eyes watered. Perched on an uncomfortable vinyl pad was no place for a big, heavy man to be hungover from whiskey. He could think of only one remedy for the smell of a bar in the morning, and the smell of his unwashed self. Before the others were up, he grabbed a bottle of Scotch from behind the bar and took a few swigs, and then a few more. He passed out again on the banquette.

Unfortunately, Matt did not change his behavior of drinking throughout the day and passing out at night. His depressed and depressing behavior continued for one full week. For most stories, the protagonist "hitting bottom" is the turning point. Drinking until passing out each night hadn't brought Matt to the bottom before. Matt would need a little extra punch to get him there.

The other people in the Forget-Me-Not Bar and Grill were concerned about Matt Early, and each had done their part to show it. Jasmine and Hymen tried to address him that first week, but when they tried, Matt turned away. Emilio, reaching out in the only way he could, made him his drinks, and looked for a sign of life in the unshaven face of the big, unhappy man. Hymen tried to feed him, and Jasmine tried to show him photos of her family back in Haiti. Paco worked the hardest to bring Matt into the fold. He talked about love, he produced sketches and drawings of fanciful motorcycles, fabulous imagined machinery, and beautiful women, clothed and unclothed, and Matt only cringed.

Thus, for one solid week, Matt did nothing but drink and pass out. At the end of the week, Emilio was in contact with State Command, pleading for them to send in a doctor. The State Command just laughed and told Emilio they had more serious problems than a drunk. Matt was going downhill fast, but he didn't have symptoms of the second wave of the virus, and neither did his fellow jail mates.

Something in his past had led Matt to this moment, the denouement of his story. In the most challenging moments of his life, Matt hadn't had the nerve to help himself out of trouble, or he found it easier to avoid situations that were too tough. Furthermore, he shunned the help, love, and guidance of other people. After all, there was plenty of booze in the world. Why should he look any further, Matt had thought, he had booze.

Matt was in a situation of classic denial, but there comes a time in a person's life when they realize something profound: that human beings, for the most part, do understand each other, when they try.

Matt's challenge was to reach out to others to help him. Matt, and those helping him, needed to look inside themselves to do so. The helpers and the helped needed to attain the grace to offer and accept that help.

There's a lesson in even the hardest experiences, such as lost loves, destroyed careers, illness, hunger (in all forms), frustrated dreams, and the disappointments that life typically offers. In short, there is a lesson in all kinds of abandonment. In human life, as in a novel, character is destiny.

Emilio was worried. He had too many tales about depressed alcoholics to tell, and this was looking like another tale. Something had to change, or Emilio would have a corpse on his hands. Emilio had enough alcohol in stock in the bar to keep Matt in booze for months; there was no denying that fact. He toyed with the idea of pouring the stock away.

Hymen was the rock they relied on, as he passed his time cooking. Whatever foodstuffs were sent in through the one window, Hymen would do something ingenious with the ingredients. And he would sing while he cooked. He had learned both in the

Merchant Marines back in Brazil. He was as tough as they came, but he could sing a love song and flip a mean burger. In contrast to Matt's morose, depressed drinking, Hymen drank beer, sang, and told off-color sailor's jokes. He tried to get a rise out of Matt, just to see if he could find some human emotion in the man.

"What you doing, man, drinking your life away? I bet you had a way with the ladies, when you were younger. Somebody done you wrong. Woman trouble? Hey—I bet she left you, didn't she? Better for you, there's more where she came from!" Hymen's eyes twinkled and he sent a few very limber pelvic thrusts in Matt's general direction.

Matt glared up at the friendly tease. "None of your biz."

But Hymen knew he had hit the mark. "That's it. Poor, big Matt, drinking because of a broken heart. You're a 'puto.' When did she leave you? Was it over your boozing? Was she screwing around when you were out drinking?"

Hymen had him. Matt jumped from his barstool and took a swing at the huge cook. There was no contest; the cook knew how to fight and had made it a regular sport on the streets of Rio when he was a kid. Hymen blocked the punch and shot a clean right jab into Matt's face. Matt went down hard, and stayed out cold for 24 hours.

Matt was a mass of blood and broken glass on the floor that night. In the morning, Matt was hurting, bleary, and needing a drink. He opened his eyes to see Emilio, Hymen, Jasmine, and Paco circled around him.

They cared, he thought in spite of himself, someone cared. Matt, who hadn't seen much of human kindness, began to whimper.

Hymen was crying like a baby. "Buddy, I didn't mean to knock you out!" Hymen grabbed Matt, and noisily embraced him, kissing him on both swollen cheeks. "I thought I killed you!"

Matt was averse to facing reality and truth, but his despair (which causes people to grow) needed to be felt. Denying it had dogged and hurt him during most of his 45 years of life.

One week of self-pity, drinking, and self-centered depression in the sealed-off Forget-Me-Not, and a hard punch, were beginning to convince Matt that he had to change. Maybe he could start small? He could try to talk with his fellow inmates. He could eat when Hymen cooked. He could find something to think about besides the booze. Hey now. What could he think about besides booze? He sat up and felt his sore jaw. A thought was beginning to form.

Booze, that was it. It was the center of his small, sad universe. So? Maybe there was something more to learn about life and booze. After all, alcohol had been around since the Egyptians and maybe before.

A light went on in Matt's head. "Emilio, how is booze made? I mean, really? Are there special blends that sell? Do you think I could experiment with distilling a Forget-Me-Not blend of booze?"

Hymen, Emilio, Jasmine, and Paco stood listening, dumbfounded. This had come straight out of left field.

Maybe it was the fact that Emilio had seen some turnarounds during his days as a bartender. Or maybe Emilio had seen enough of life in 80 plus years that he believed in hope. Maybe he was just a fool. But Emilio jumped at the chance to help.

"Have you noticed how vicarious pleasure works?" he said to Matt. "It is allows people to see their story from the outside, just like a narrator does for the characters in a novel. You just might taper down your intake, Matt, if you find something creative. Yes, create a story or an endeavor related to your habit. Why do you think an old alcoholic like me opened a bar after years under my belt as a bartender? Why do you think that skinny people like to feed others? Why do you think that shrinks tell people how to live?"

Maybe, thought Emilio, he was advising Matt to do the kind of thing he had done when he opened the Forget-Me-Not. Emilio was an old alcoholic around booze every day. Maybe Matt, too, could find something drinking-related that wasn't just passive drinking. Emilio, at that moment, had a brilliant thought, and said, "I have some cheap wine back there, Matt. I've been saving it since 2008 to try my hand at making a tonic or an Italian-style fortified wine. I will rig up a distiller, and together we can try to make a fortified wine, like we did back in Italy. And you can see what we have in the kitchen to add to the blend."

Matt was listening. The wheels in his head were turning, and Emilio could see that.

"Maybe you'll discover a Forget-Me-Not blend. I always wanted to do that," Emilio said. "And now we have the time, you have the time, and you have nothing left to lose. Yes, you have nothing left to lose. Nothing. This is your one shot." Emilio couldn't help himself. He continued, "My God, man. Make something. Create something. A man can't live without creating something."

Hymen, listening and watching, began to cry. He was witnessing a moment when another human being sees something bigger than himself.

On the ninth day of confinement, Emilio and Matt set up a makeshift still in the kitchen. Hymen helped find the cases of cheap old red wine in the back room, lifting them three at a time. Emilio rigged up a vessel for heating the wine, and improvised a condenser.

The first small batch smelled very potent indeed. Then came the biggest question that Matt had ever asked in all his 45 years: "What are we going to add, to make it a true Forget-Me-Not blend?"

He addressed this question to the other four, seeking their help and advice. Emilio, in the wisdom of his years, said, "What do you want to do, Matt?"

Matt thought about the three things he loved most in his life: booze, chocolate, and vanilla ice cream. "What the hell," he said to Emilio, as Hymen looked on with tears in his eyes. "I'd like to throw in some sugar, some cocoa beans, and some vanilla extract—and then we'll cook it again. What the hell. We have time. Plenty of time, in fact. Four and a half more weeks. And we have each other. We can do this together."

Jasmine and Paco heard this, emerged from various corners of the Forget-Me-Not, and joined the grand experiment in the kitchen. They were the first to taste the big booze project that would eventually be called "Forget Me Never." It was an American-Italian style fortified red wine, with Sicilian flavoring, and it would make the Forget-Me-Not Bar and Grill famous. Although no one knew it yet, the project would make all five of them significant money. The fortified wine that Matt and the others created would be the hallmark of Emilio's bar and legacy.

Matt Early smiled at Emilio, Hymen, little Jasmine, and the great lover Paco, and said, "Well, that's just the first batch. It'll get better, just you wait..."

Chapter 7

The "Perfect Brown" Hair Dye

I f a bouffant coiffure could spout forth steam, Nancy Jean's beehive hairdo would have been smoking. Had Elaine D. Jones been one of those people who is usually a smidge late, Nancy Jean would not have been trapped in a small beauty salon with that irritating woman. Thanks to Elaine's compulsive promptness, Nancy Jean, owner of the Golden Pin-Up Salon, was now stuck in 42 days of quarantine with a client she had never relished.

Both silently brooding, the two women had suffered through their own private turmoil during the first five hours of lockdown at the Pin. Five hours had now passed since the smaller woman's Monitor Bracelet had sprung into action, with flashing red lights and commands from the State. Three women sat solidly on beauty chairs in a locked-down midwestern beauty salon. One of them napped (Denise); two women simmered in silence, dwelling upon the injustices of their respective lives that had led them to this point. Elaine and Nancy Jean viewed the impending forced confinement of 42 days as further proof that life, unpredictable and unreliable as it was, consistently and inconveniently inserted itself into one's orderly plans.

The Pin was an average salon in a long, narrow retail space in a 1920s Tudor revival building in Topeka. The front bay window was about eight feet across, with little English-style glazed panes. Looking out to Frenchman's Cove Avenue, the window gazed at the Mission Outreach Thrift Store and Homeless Food Bank, which occupied a converted Sears building. Topeka had changed, and, at the time of the Crisis, the Golden Pin-Up was on the good side of the change, and right across the street was the bad side.

Down the length of the Pin, there were three 1980s beauty chairs, newly reupholstered in maroon Leatherette, arranged in a row. In the first chair, closest to the bay window, Nancy Jean Hammily reclined uneasily, her thin but strong arms crossed over her smallish breasts. Her chin, which usually was held quite high, was pinned to her clavicle, and her high heels were crossed on the footrest of the beauty chair. Her makeup was flawless, and her big hair was sprayed into place, even after so vehemently venting her anger at Elaine. She was steaming mad, and she looked it. She had to think of a plan. A plan to keep order in the face of disorder, a plan to fill the prospect of unstructured time, that empty, liminal time and space known as quarantine.

In the next chair down the line, Denise Bustamante's head, with its short bob of dark straight hair, rested on the seat back and rolled in the direction of the thrift store and food bank. A little smear of chocolate flitted across her upper lip, too close to her nose to lick off, even if she had been awake. She had fallen asleep 20 minutes after her Monitor Bracelet told her she would be locked down with her boss and Elaine D. Jones for 42 days. Denise could fall asleep anywhere, anytime. Her relaxed attitude toward life allowed her to maintain a good appetite and sleep restfully at night. Her body now exhibited the peaceful abandonment of a regular napper. In fact, Denise slept her way through most of the 42 days, as sleeping was her favorite occupation.

Elaine D. Jones sat in the third beauty chair from the window. Elaine was a study in continuous thought, her petite 60-plus face working itself into an infant-like mewling, then into a nervous twittering snigger, and finally into little grins of satisfaction. Elaine's face typically showed exactly what she was thinking and feeling, although she was unaware that other people could read her; she would have been horrified to be thought of as transparent. Elaine was relieved to have received a pass-card out of her life for a while.

She was a principled woman who fit the mold of most conservative midwestern ladies of a certain age. She had no children to change her mind about the Young People of Today, and no ex-husband to convince her that all men were evil. She had Bernard, of course, but he was hardly more noticeable than the wall-to-wall carpet in her practical and efficient home on Rockland Place. He was impossible, an unabashed freethinker of the most harmless kind, which, to Elaine, was the most annoying kind of all.

Elaine, who had never changed an opinion in her life, was about to be faced with an opportunity to change, and the change would come through Nancy Jean. Nancy Jean was deep in thought, searching her mind for something to occupy their time, for a plan to put into action. Nothing frightens women who like order as much as free time.

To be free with time, friendship, money; to be free with the natural flow of life, to re-invent oneself, was a freedom untried by both Nancy Jean and Elaine. Elaine did not want to change anything about herself (except her gray roots!). Her favorite song was Sinatra's "My Way," and she kept her way to herself. Elaine was cautious about anyone knowing her financial situation, meager as it was, or anyone thinking she had too fine a taste. She dressed in clothing from the former Sears and JC Penney. Her car was a VW Passat, very middle of the road. She didn't buy anything expensive, and when she took short vacations with Bernard, it was somewhere where everyone else could have gone, like Canada or Florida. Bernard loved the beach; Elaine found beaches messy.

Elaine sat in the beauty chair, looking squarely at her black pumps, and thought, instead, about Frank Sinatra. Now there was a man, The Chairman, the solid important type of man she should have married. He made the rules. She liked people who made rules. Of course, the bigger the rule-maker, the more important the rules, so she had a great respect for the heads of banks, heads of State, fathers, rental agents and condo managers, and all authority figures in general.

People who she chose to allow into her life simply had to believe, like her, that structure and order were the main goals in life. It did not matter what held that structure together; force of will held Elaine's structured life together. Order was the main thing. Bernard, she thought, as she studied her pumps, was so tolerant, so flexible, that one didn't know where one stood with him. Elaine was looking forward to a Bernard-free 42 days. He caused such messes. Stacks of *New Yorker* magazines, unread for months, unopened mail, solicitations from Save the Children, Save the Whales, and that kind of thing. His whole life is chaos, she thought. She was glad to be able to think clearly, without overhearing Bernard on the phone organizing poetry readings for his old hippie friends.

Elaine was the kind of woman who kept her check registers in a dated file and her spoons nestled together in the drawer. She was a lover of instruction manuals, guidebooks, maps, and modestly priced cookbooks. When she made a recipe and found that the cookbook called for too much of an ingredient, she would make a note in pencil in that erroneous cookbook, thereby exercising her own order upon it.

She did have her hair colored, as it was getting gray, but even that slight attempt at breaking the rules of natural hair was not followed to extremes. This fateful morning, she had gone into the Pin to have a little brown dye applied over the gray, as she did once every two months. Fate, which always sends us the most interesting situations, had placed Elaine in a salon where women came to be "done-up." Look at Nancy Jean and her bouffant and make-up! She was quarantined in a hall of superfluous artifice. Elaine wished that Fate could have placed her in an accountant's office or a stock investment ladies' club. People might think, she thought to herself, when this is all over, that I'm the showy type of woman that spends money on hairdressers. That would be too much. How we perceive others versus how others perceive us was the conflict that Fate had in store for Nancy Jean and Elaine, and Fate could not have chosen a better place to do this than a beauty salon.

Nancy Jean, indeed, enjoyed her elaborate bouffant coiffure, dyed very deep matte brown, paired with too much make-up, unlike Elaine's modest, practical bob and "natural" lipstick. But both women shared a love of structure. Being seen as practical, organized, and reserved was much more valued than being free and easy, especially free and easy with money or time.

As they began the quarantine together, Nancy Jean wanted to make the rules clear to Elaine. "One thing we must get straight right away: I keep my salon perfect. And now we are quarantined, I expect you to toe the line. Any dish you use, you wash it. No dishes in the sink, no water glasses on the tables. I want each towel used to be placed immediately in the hamper. I want each hairbrush to be in the sterilizer. I do not tolerate disorder. This is my salon and I am captain of the ship. Denise will not be much help; she'll sleep all day if we let her. You and I will manage only if you follow my rules. Do I make myself clear?"

"Well!" Elaine replied, obviously surprised to hear Nancy Jean speak, finally. "Well. You are very clear." She set her small upper lip into a very straight line. She continued, petulantly, "So you will watch my every move. I know what it is like to be watched and judged, and I suspect someone watched you and judged you. I don't like walking on eggshells for anyone." Elaine's voice broke. "I bet a man had something to do with all this watching and judging! I bet a man disordered your life!"

Elaine was right. Although Nancy Jean didn't deign to answer Elaine, she fell into a reverie arisen by this accusation. Nancy Jean was in charge in her salon, the only place she had ever felt powerful, because of the chaos and disorder in her past life. Living under a domineering father, she had decided to marry the first man who showed interest. What a looker he was and how romantic he was! He could talk to anyone and seemed so easy-going. He was a promising young medical student, and her father had approved. He gave them a little money and a VW Bug to help them start their lives together. So, she ran to the altar and left her studies at beauty school.

Medical school was a challenge for her young husband, and her young groom stumbled over his studies. Nancy Jean brought him his nightly dinner, and then, watching him doze over his physiology books, she took pity on him and put him to bed. She would then finish his homework and write his papers and organize his work for the morning. He was carried through three years of medical school by Nancy Jean.

After his residency, her young husband left her for a much younger receptionist at the hospital. He told Nancy Jean that he had found a woman who made him feel like a man, who looked up to him, and who didn't make him feel inadequate. Left without money, and without much faith in herself, Nancy Jean crawled back to her dad, who lay all the blame on Nancy Jean.

Nancy Jean hated to do so, but she begged her dad for money to open a salon. Smart, focused, and orderly, she had never looked back. In later life, she was lonely, so she married again; not to a fun-loving, immature boy, but to a serious, weighty older man, who, in time, spoke to her and judged her as her father had. At home, that is. Not in her salon.

Nancy Jean had made the Golden Pin-Up a success, she thought, and smiled to herself as she reflected on this triumph over the vicissitudes of the men in her life. She was not going to let a 42-day quarantine with spineless, simple, strait-laced Elaine force her back into a world of cowering weakness. Her own self-esteem was tied to her salon, her life, her business. In her space she was her own boss, the most important member of the small staff, and she called all the shots. To sink herself into the management and order of the place was her solace from anyone who had doubted her power and intelligence. And this little person, with her short little bob, her little organized handbag, and her small views on the world was not going to take that away.

Nancy Jean, faced with the unknown for 42 days, felt the need to create a plan of order. But with what? Forty-two days here together, thought Nancy Jean, with only the contents of the salon to manipulate. What could she do to structure life for this quarantine? Through the execution of her plan, although it was not her intention, she would begin to understand Elaine, and through this understanding, she would begin to see herself. Her plan was forming, and it was called "The Perfect Brown."

The Perfect Brown was to be her quest, aided by Elaine as assistant, to find the right proportions of the right formula for the most elusive of all hair colors, the natural-looking brown, the anathema of all color processes for a master beautician. Brown, although the most prevalent of all hair colors, was the hardest to mimic, as if natural, because it was not natural. Brown contained all colors within its hues, and was the hardest to perfect in art.

The majority of color clientele at the Pin believed in the honesty of a brown head of hair. Blondes were sluts, redheads were foolish and frivolous and hot tempered and passionate, black-haired women were harlots and jezebels, yet brunettes were solid people who took vows seriously. In short, hair color mattered and made the character of the woman come to life.

What's in a name? Brown was Nancy Jean's most requested color. Nancy Jean's clients asked for brown dye colors by trade-names established at the dawn of commercial dye manufacture: a dark brown beige is known as "Sweet Little Latte," the light red-gold brown hue is called "Strawberry Cream Soda," and the medium copper brown hue is named "Firelight in Fall." Brown is not one color; it is a range of personalities accomplished through art.

In her head, Nancy Jean developed the parameters of The Perfect Brown, a quest that naturally would require an artist and a model, yet would take advantage of established rules of chemistry, known measurements, and the precise weighing out of ingredients. Nancy Jean had always wanted to undertake such an elusive goal. Few beauticians are ever completely satisfied with a processed brown head of hair for a particular woman. This idea, thought Nancy Jean, was perfect in itself. It would give a sense of order to the long days under lockdown, and she would be the boss, the master manipulator, the artist in charge! Elaine would be the subject.

Nancy Jean, gathering up her firmest in-control voice, proposed her plan to Elaine, who was lost in pleasant thoughts about balancing the checkbook located in her bag, as she sat in the beauty chair next to Nancy Jean.

"Elaine," said Nancy Jean. "We are going to master the chemical process of The Perfect Brown. Brown is the hardest color to get right. Brown is complex, subtle, and has within it hues and tones of red or blue. I can make you into an ash brown brunette with a bluish tone or a copper brown brunette with a reddish tone. If I was not a talented operator, I could give you purple hair, or bright orange. I could fry your hair off your head in the quest for the right brown, if I didn't know what I was doing. It comes down to the right measurements, the right proportions, the right order, the right timing." Elaine was listening with rapt attention. She heard the words she loved: order, proportion, measurements.

"You have straight fine hair," Nancy Jean continued. "That kind of hair doesn't absorb color as easily as my hair, which has a natural curl. Curly hair sucks up color. What that means is that if I am to find your perfect brown, I create a color mix away from the warmer hues, away from the red tones. Fine hair like yours doesn't absorb color easily, so any brown it sucks up will turn out warmer when dry. That's why for your hair, I might add a little ash tone, a bluer hue, to create a perfect brown. My curly hair, which sucks up color, needs the mix to include more warmth, more red tones, to create a perfect brown."

This mutual quest, therefore, began on that very first day of quarantine in a small room called the Color Bar at the Pin, where both women felt equally empowered amongst the measuring cups, measuring bowls, measuring spoons, and calibrated bottles. The activity gave them both a feeling of control that they needed and wanted, and they slowly developed a friendship that would last well after the 42 days of quarantine.

"Elaine, we'll begin with you," Nancy Jean said in her commanding voice. "You have straight fine hair, so we'll pick a shade of medium brown—104 by L'Oréal, "Caramel Temptation"—and add ash tone, about five-sixths of a tablespoon. Now we use three-quarters of a tablespoon of black without a red undertone, and when we add the proper mix of developer, it will compensate for your straight fine hair, which tends to absorb less true brown.

"Now, we'll add a little less developer than recommended for a woman with color-absorbing hair, say, one-sixth of a cup, and because your hair is shoulder length, we compute the developer in proportion to the increased volume of dye. We mix it in a plastic bowl, because metal will oxidize the dye and you'll end up with orange or purple hair."

Was Elaine overwhelmed by fractions? Was she lost in the proportions and the orderly progression of steps? On the contrary, Elaine was well practiced at precise measurements, as evidenced in her cookbooks with personalized marginalia of corrections to the printed recipes. Elaine was sucking up Nancy Jean's orderly procedures as fast as curly hair sucks up dye. In fact, her little mouth, typical turned down at the corners, formed a round "O" of fascination and delight.

"This is exactly the kind of thing I excel at, Nancy Jean!" Elaine said, referring to her partner-in-quarantine on a first name basis for the first time in 16 years. "I love measurements! I've got to write this down for history's sake. I'll be your model and secretary. When may I try a perfect brown on you?"

Nancy Jean stiffened her spine. "Elaine. Hair color is a science. You are not a beautician. A processed, complex color, most especially brown, is a delicate mixture. You can try your first mixture on me in a few days, but I will supervise. You will split the hair on my head in four sections with four clips of the same size. You will keep notes, and soon, we will vote on our perfect brown. We will override nature, which fades us all into gray. We'll take control of our future!"

Elaine rose to the challenge. In the second week of quarantine, Elaine became so good at mixing the chemicals that she began to experiment. She learned that she could mitigate dry ends of long hair by retaining three tablespoons of dye in the bowl mixed with two tablespoons of shampoo, to be added to the ends exactly three minutes before rinsing the whole head. This washed the ends in a sheen of color, but did not dry them further, an important addition when each woman was trying on a new perfect brown every two days.

Even Nancy Jean was impressed, and ventured a smile at Elaine in the third week of quarantine. Elaine created a system for muting an aggressive brown by applying deep conditioner to Nancy Jean's damp hair, wrapping her head in plastic wrap, further wrapping the head in a hot towel. At exactly ten minutes into the wrapping process, Elaine hit Nancy Jean with a hot blow dryer to keep the process warm. After ten more minutes, she shampooed and reconditioned. And her matte lifeless brown morphed into The Perfect Brown!

As a treat, on the 20th day of experimentation, each woman dried the other woman's brown creation under a bonnet dryer, and they styled each other's hair. So coiffed, the women sat down to dinner, at which seating each woman arranged their own set of cutlery to line up perfectly. Nancy Jean doled out portions that were not too much of anything on each woman's plate.

They felt bolstered up enough to enjoy the State-catered food (thankfully wine was included that day). They gave each other a small complement, which no one would have thought was too much (because too much praise is phony if you are a practical, orderly sort of woman).

"How nice that shade of brown is on you, my dear!" Then they toasted the day, and each other, and brought out their notes on measurements and proportions, and, comparing notes, they dined.

90

Chapter 8

Mrs. Folger Tells a Parrot Joke

L uck takes many different forms, and one is giving you what you didn't want but needed. A dental example might be that a small thought, like a small cavity, may turn into quite a big thought, and a large infection. All good dentists know that when plaque begins, it is the start of something ominous.

You can floss, and brush more observantly, and gargle with Chlorhexidine Gluconate 0.12%, but the plaque may creep and become gingivitis. Then, instead of an oral rinse, a good dentist will realize it is time to get out the power tools and do a scaling. The dentist must cause and be caused some pain for the pleasure of the future.

Dr. Randolph Edwards, before his Monitor Bracelet flashed red, had been wishing that he would get lucky. Ms. Morgantown, the embodiment of the plaque metaphor herself, had been in his chair at the time. Elisa Morgantown, a lithe and toned 30-year-old horsewoman, had come in that Tuesday before lunch with a chipped canine. If Dr. Edwards's bracelet had not flashed just as Mrs. Folger had come in with the X-rays, he would have discovered that Elisa needed a filling.

And if his monitor had not exploded in color and commands, Dr. Edwards would have had a very satisfied smile on his face. He would have discovered a cavity that was simple to remedy, and the filling would have required another visit by Ms. Morgantown. He then would have used his depth sounder, that torturous dental tool, to help him find what professionals call a pocket, close to six millimeters deep, located at Ms. Morgantown's beautiful bicuspid.

This discovery would have thrilled him because a third appointment would be required, and more in the future to monitor that pocket.

If undetected, what would be the result of that pocket for the dental health of Elisa Morgantown? That pocket, left unchecked to cause plaque in the area, would spread its contagion to other areas of her delicate and tender pink mouth, and she would be a likely candidate for gingivitis. Thus, unchecked, the small could become the large.

As in biology, also in life: when something begins that is likely to fester, severe measures need to be taken to halt future—and bigger—problems. And sometimes you need luck to step in and stop the problem while it's small.

Dr. Edwards had a suburban life with his wife, Trisk, and three children, and had many manly hobbies, such as cleaning and collecting antique rifles. When he first ushered Ms. Morgantown into his office five months before for a cleaning, he realized his life had been too small for a virile dentist like himself. And, like something in the mouth that goes bad, his obsession with her beauty festered, and he began to picture Ms. Morgantown in other positions beside supine on the six-thousand-dollar Ritter dental chair.

As luck—or perhaps fate—would have it, Dr. Edwards was locked in place with the charming Elisa, and with the late-middle-aged, reliable and efficient Mrs. Folger. One female entity he welcomed, and the other, he regretted. Oh, had Mrs. Folger just stayed a few minutes longer watering the philodendron in the little girls' room, he might have been locked in place alone with a 30-year-old natural beauty!

But the Fates, who are also female, know a thing or two about men. And so they threw Mrs. Folger into the lockdown too, just to clarify to Dr. Edwards that although women can be pliable, young, fresh, and beautiful, they can also be strong, in control, and firm—like a grandmother.

Once their bracelets stopped flashing, Dr. Edwards said, "Well, Ms. Morgantown, looks like we are quarantined together. Shall we start by getting out of that chair and rinsing?" He de-bibbed Elisa and moved to remove his white lab coat.

Mrs. Folger had just reinstalled the philodendron on the office window ledge in front of the foam quarantine sealant. Suddenly, she appeared at the door and said, "I think we will leave our lab coat on, Dr. Edwards, as I believe you have not begun your pocket measurements on the gum below that chipped canine, which you know you always do in cases like this. I suggest we get the whole mouth for our records."

Mrs. Folger was clear. This quarantine was to be all business. And no funny business.

"We have three more teeth, and after we finish we can break for lunch. Luckily I brought enough lunch for three," Mrs. Folger said. She always had enough food to get her through 12 hours.

Ms. Morgantown, who had spat into the round bowl and could speak clearly, said, "What did you bring? I love homemade sandwiches!" She smiled at the matronly Mrs. Folger. "Did you bring any cookies?'

"Ham and Swiss on rye, and I can provide three chocolate milks from the lab fridge," she said. "The paperwork from State Command says that as of tonight they will provide meals delivered through the one window that has been left unsealed. So thank goodness we have lunch."

Ms. Morgantown said, "The way Dr. Edwards's stomach was growling, he needs that ham and cheese." She giggled like a child.

This was excruciating for Dr. Edwards. Not only was he under Mrs. Folger's thumb, his stomach had betrayed him as neither a bon vivant nor a Don Juan, but a human male. Biology again, setting forth an obvious truth, hidden in a digestive growl. Dr. Edwards looked ashamed and inflamed by lust. Mrs. Folger looked at him disapprovingly; she helped Elisa to her feet, showed her to the office's diminutive toilet and sink, and suggested lunch would be served in Dr. Edwards's office.

Dr. Edwards's office had been designed by Trisk, his talented wife. Believing that all dental offices should convey the modernity of the profession, she had used modern tones, with a large glass desk. There were no visible filing cabinets, weighty computers or printers, notepads, Post-it note containers, staplers, or tape dispensers. No, all the trappings of an office were hidden behind the back wall, in front of which was a modern, Eames-style black leather and chrome office chair.

The office desk was a single piece of heavy modern plate glass, in an amoebic shape, with a single tubular chrome support. The desk's only design feature was a collection of colorful flecked Italian paperweights of all sizes, glass globes in primary colors that lit up the surface of the clear glass desktop.

On the side wall was a Ball State Dental School diploma, and various other trophies, such as a marksman's award and the Paul Harris from the Rotary Club. The office was masculine, with an imitation zebra rug on the fake hardwood floor to reference that Dr. Edwards liked to hunt. Two chairs for consultations were ranged in front of the desk. They were gray leather, very low, in the Barcelona style, with arms and back slung together with tubular steel struts.

Not cheap, the whole design. Modern, manly, black and white. Trisk had done a perfect dental office. She spent fifteen thousand on high-end furniture, but she had saved on the interior designer because she did it herself.

Mrs. Folger had always disapproved of the hard edge of Dr. Edwards's office. That day, she made her point in a symbolic gesture. She had a pink crocheted lace shawl in her reticule that would serve as a tablecloth for lunch. She threw it over the manly, modern, expensive desk. Dr. Edwards was surprised to see his desk draped in pink acrylic crochet when he came in from the toilet. Elisa and Mrs. Folger were chatting about crochet techniques.

During lunch, Dr. Edwards sat behind his desk, in a position of control. Dentists frown as they sit behind their desks, preparing to tell patients how much a procedure might cost. Not being trained as businessmen in dental school, dentists frown because they believe professional medical people should not talk money. Dr. Edwards struck this same frowning posture behind his ham and Swiss.

Trisk never used cheap mustard, only the fancy Boar's Head stuff. Here he was looking at the sickly yellow of French's on Mrs. Folger's homemade sandwiches. Straight out of a yellow plastic squeeze bottle, he imagined, which likely had ketchup stains on it.

The women were seated with handkerchiefs over their laps in front of his manly desk. Lest his imagination run wild about mustard, he asked them, "Heard any good jokes lately?"

Mrs. Folger was a good sport for all her professionalism, and was known to tell a few off-color jokes at the dental office's annual Christmas party. "Oh yes!" she said, "the captain of Bob's bowling team told Bob a good one last week, but it has some swear words in it. I hope that's okay with Ms. Morgantown." Bob was her long-suffering husband, who was about to retire from his construction job with the electric company.

"Oh, I swear sometimes, too!" Ms. Morgantown nodded her head rapidly many times to indicate that she did not mind swear words in the least.

Mrs. Folger replied, "Good girl. And this joke is so perfect, because it's about a deep freeze."

Mrs. Folger was no poet, but she had made the connection between the 42-day quarantine looming before them and a deep freeze. Dr. Edwards thought a little like a poet of the Romantic era, who turned all situations into thwarted sex. However, at first he didn't get Mrs. Folger's metaphorical connection. After considering it for a minute, he realized that the metaphor was dismaying to him.

If he could get Ms. Morgantown alone, perhaps in the toilet, he would show her that this quarantine didn't have to be a deep freeze, he thought. At the thought of exhibiting something warm to Ms. Morgantown in the bathroom, he broke into a wide, wicked smile.

"Do continue with your joke, Mrs. Folger," he said. "We don't have all day." He stopped and looked up.

Ms. Morgantown said, "Oh, yes we do!" and giggled enough for three girls.

Mrs. Folger looked with benign condescension at Ms. Morgantown, for it was becoming obvious that she was simple. She began to tell her joke. "A man inherited a rare old parrot from a relative he knew nothing about. One day the parrot and a huge cage were delivered with a note that said: 'This is from your great uncle, bequeathing this bird to you. Please take care of him.'

"The man took the large and beautiful bird into his small apartment, and fed him, and gave him water and a spray bath every day. The bird grew angry at the spray bath each day and increasingly hated the spray bottle. He snapped at the bottle one day and said, 'You jerk supreme. You disgrace to humanity. You little shidict. You dog. You cretin. You runny glob of mucus.' And so on.

"The bird's owner was dumbfounded. 'What did you say?' he asked the bird, who stood defiant, defending himself against the spray bottle. The bird repeated his nasty oaths.

"'I have had enough,' said the owner, and he opened the big cage door, pulled the bird out, took him to the deep freeze, and threw him in."

Ms. Morgantown, an animal lover, began to whimper and choke. Her reaction to the joke said a lot about her mental capacity, and also illustrated that behind a beautiful, well-constructed exterior may lie a less well-constructed mind. " don't like that joke, Mrs. Folger, take it baaaaack!" she cried.

Mrs. Folger, surprised but in charge, said, "Don't be silly, Ms. Morgantown, this is make believe. It is a joke, which by the way is not finished yet. So stop whining and listen, it's funny!"

Taking her handkerchief from her lap, Ms. Morgantown blew her nose. Like some demure and beautiful women do, Ms. Morgantown had the loudest honk when she blew her nose. Dr. Edwards looked surprised. Such a sound from such a little button of a nose!

Mrs. Folger continued her joke, undaunted. "The bird's owner, having thrown the bird in the deep freeze, walked around his tiny apartment twice. Then he approached the deep freeze, reached in, and pulled the bird out of the cold. The bird, only a little frozen, looked up with grateful eyes at his owner, and said, 'Oh, dear owner, dear man, dear provider. I will never swear at you again. The punishment was terrible, so now I have learned my lesson. Thank you.'

"The owner said to his bird, 'I know you're only a bird, and you must have been taught those words, so I forgive you.'

"The bird said to his owner, 'I am glad we are friends again. And as a friend, I must ask you one question, and then we will put this whole sordid incident behind us.'

"The owner replied, 'Ask away.'

"'Just tell me,' said the parrot, 'what did the chicken do?'"

In spite of himself, Dr. Edwards, snorted and then laughed. Some of the Swiss cheese got up his nose, so he snorted again to try to cover it up.

Mrs. Folger, who loved her own jokes, howled with laughter. Her large bosom and ample tummy shook, and she laughed so hard at her own joke that the bread fell off her sandwich. She laughed so hard that her glasses slid down her large nose. She laughed so hard that she began to weep.

Ms. Morgantown, on the other hand, did not crack a smile and did not laugh. She looked vapid, hurt, and confused. "What chicken? I thought he was a parrot." She continued, in a little girl voice, with, "Thank God the bird was okay, anyway, after spending five minutes in a deep freeze. I would not have liked that either, that poor bird. People do the most horrible things to pets. I once had a stable hand who tortured his pet cockroaches. I once had a trainer who raised rabbits and ate them. I once had a mucker who hunted. Who would be such a bully as to aim a gun at an innocent animal?" She looked at Dr. Edwards with her huge blue eyes and said, "I could never love anyone who had aimed a gun at an animal."

She turned to Mrs. Folger. "But about the joke, Mrs. Folger. What do you mean about a chicken? Where does a chicken come in?"

Dr. Edwards thought about his intelligent wife. She could put together a dinner or an office, run her business, and play bridge. He felt certain that Trisk would have understood the chicken in question to have been a package of meat in the deep freeze. Then he remembered the early-morning showers where he had run through all the beautiful patients in his files and picked Ms. Morgantown as the one who had the most promise.

He realized that something that begins as small as a cavity, such as a little thought of dalliance with a patient, can inflate into quite a confusing sexual head trip. The occasional wafts of second-hand nitrous oxide he breathed had nothing on his flights of fancy regarding the beautiful body of Elisa Morgantown. But what of the mind of a woman? What weight should a virile 45-year-old man give to the mind of a woman after whom he lusts?

He knew he was stuck with that perfectly formed body for 42 days, and he tried to forgive her lack of intelligence and comprehension, as demonstrated by her reaction to the joke. With that simple joke's punch line that she had failed to grasp, he had come crashing down to earth.

Sitting in his leather office chair, he was fighting with himself. He was a man, but also a man of science who valued intelligence. Not everyone is Einstein, he wavered. However, given 42 days with a beautiful body or 42 days with a beautiful mind, he knew which he would choose, or he thought he did. He tried to reason like the dentist God had created him to be. He mused into his ham and Swiss. There's nothing like a beautiful mind. Nothing at all.

And then, as he thought for another minute, he smiled and mumbled aloud,

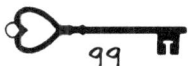

"Although a nice rack does come close…"

Mrs. Folger, on the other side of the amoeba-shaped glass desk, was alerted by the doctor's wicked smile and the unmistakable word "rack." She began to stand, very slowly, and then she reached across that desk for a heavy paperweight.

ELIZABETH STEWART

101

Chapter 9

BMW Munich Delivers

The Finance Department at Sterling BMW in Newport Beach, California, was a dreary, out-of-date, airless place to envision 42 days of seclusion. Manny's Monitor Bracelet had erupted at the apex of an arc made by his burly arm and attached fist as he drew back in preparation for a punch. His fist was aimed at the meek George Smithson, director of finance for Sterling BMW. George was almost completely hidden under the chipped brown 1970s Formica desk that he had called his workstation for 15 years.

In the minute that had elapsed since both bracelets flashed red, and Command crackled out its orders, George's head, with its thinning grayish comb-over on top, inched its way up to peer over the edge of the desk. He wanted to have a good look at his new and frightening "office-mate," Manny Nichols.

As the two men were beginning to emerge, one from anger, and one from under his desk, the Foam Insulation Rig was blasting a coating around the finance office door. The clank of the power blaster was interesting to Manny, who cocked an ear, and said, "State Crew should get that engine looked over. The alternator's going."

Manny was one of those mechanical engineers who has a literal outlook on the world. If you make a comment of a non-engineering bent, this kind of engineer will put the comment through the computer in his head, with checks for accuracy and strength of the facts. Thus, all innocent observations directed to this type of engineer have a resonance that falls beneath the more poetic meanings of words. For example, if you casually mentioned, "Oh would you look! The sky is completely blue today," and then smiled at Manny, he would look around and respond, "No, the sky is not completely blue. It has a few small clouds, and furthermore, even if the sky appeared completely blue, with the nature of air currents, you are bound to be wrong over time."

George Smithson, on the other hand, was deep, introverted, timid, kind, and very quiet.

George, born in Craft City, Nevada, didn't know his father past age 11. Until he was 20 and left for college, George's great aunt had told him often that his father, Frank, was everything that George would never be. Frank was tall and athletic. He grew up in St. Louis and swam the Mississippi with his five virile brothers at the age of 16. He was too young to fight when Word War II erupted, so he joined the Canadian Mounties and shipped over. Frank joined the Mounties because he was an expert horseman, and because of this skill, he made an excellent transition to the Army Motorcycle Corps. Old pictures held dear by George's mother showed Frank on a vintage army bike in tall (sexy) black boots. When Frank returned from the war, he married Mrs. Smithson.

Frank was accepted into the St. Louis police department as a sergeant, and because he had no vices, he was made head of narcotics. There he tailed truly bad apples and because his job was so hush-hush, he could never tell George exactly what he did. George was invited to join his dad on other ventures, none of which suited George's delicate and precise ways. Frank tried to teach George model railroad electronics and track building, car mechanics, photo enlarging, and target practice with a very frightening (to George) handgun from the War.

Frank's toolboxes, attic, and garage were filled with power machines and wool hats with flaps to go over the ears. He worked outside on projects when he was not capturing drug lords coming down the Mississippi River. He died when one of the most notorious drug lords came up from New Orleans, and Frank, who had boarded the drug-laden Chris Craft, was tossed overboard into the river. At that point he was 50 years old, and he didn't make it to the other side as he was reported to have done when he was 16.

George grew up inadequate, small, blonde, of thin face and small hand. Instead of the large tools that spoke to his dad, small tools like slide rules, microscopes, and jewelry-making kits enticed George. He wanted to be a microbiologist, but he was afraid of germs, so he trained as a CPA. His minor at University of Nevada was 18th-century English Literature, and he loved John Donne and Robert Herrick. He knew many poems, lost in the sands of time, by heart. When he couldn't sleep, which was most nights, he recited,

> *"Since I am coming to that holy room,*
>> *Where, with thy choir of saints for evermore,*
> *I shall be made thy music; as I come*
>> *I tune the instrument here at the door,*
>> *And what I must do then, think here before."*

Almost everything about the human touch concerned George. He wouldn't shake hands for fear of germs, he wouldn't dine out for fear of hands on his plate, and he wouldn't use a public restroom because he knew what men's hands hold in men's restrooms. This last was such a phobia that for years he urinated in a hospital bottle in his car (which was not a BMW) while parked in the lot at Sterling. That is, he urinated in his car until Mr. Sterling caught him, and then Mr. Sterling was forced to build George his own bathroom, a completely enclosed unit, attaching to the finance office.

George's solace was online bridge (real cards might carry germs); he could use his analytic mind to the fullest extent. Numbers were clean, carried no disease, and were reliable. And numbers had their own poetry, their own art. George had a brain condition called color-graphemic synesthesia, which caused him to perceive numbers as inherently colored. So, when George thought with numbers, his world lit up in color. Nothing else in George's meager life lit the world up in color; only numbers. Each number also had its own odor, for George.

So, you see his job in finance at Sterling BMW was a bit of an escape from the germ-laden world. But not always. When George was faced with a new client across the brown Formica desk, his imagination ran away with him before he could talk himself down; he saw where their hands had been. This was especially gut wrenching if the client had been shown to the restroom before they were ushered in to sign paperwork with George. And that was the worst: the signing.

When a client came in to sign finance papers, George was to produce a custom-made Sterling Writing Instrument made by Parker and engraved across the shaft, "A 100% Sterling Purchase: A Sterling BMW." When George pumped the contract out of his ancient printer, the client would sign his name and then would be asked to hand the pen to George. Mr. Sterling had insisted that George sign for the dealership, so George would receive the germ-infested Sterling Pen from the new owner of the shiny BMW, and he would sign the bottom of the contract. It was all George could do to keep his shirt on each time a client handed him the pen. He would itch all over because of the germs on the pen. This was why George only wore bow ties; they kept his shirt on him.

We had a classic combination of two very different men emerging as a pair inside the Sterling BMW Finance Department: an angry engineer and a timid and nervous numbers guy.

Manny had plonked himself onto the black vinyl chair in front of George's desk, and was glaring at George. George resumed his seat at his desk and looked down at his cuticles.

"Well, what the hell are we going to do for 42 days, you piss-ant little jerk?" Manny hissed at George.

George's office phone rang. It was Mr. Sterling, and he was beside himself. "You always bring me bad luck, Smithson. Now I have no head of finance for 42 days. Now I have foam all over my plate glass windows in the hall by your office. Now I have to hire someone to open the door for your stupid meals. You probably knew this was going to happen. I told you not to accept Nichols's lease back, and look what you do. You force the State to lock you up so you won't have to face me! Well, you have another surprise coming, buddy boy. You are going to face the future, and the future is coming this afternoon. Check the intraoffice schedule, you nitwit. A present is coming to finance." And with that, Mr. Sterling slammed down the phone.

"What the fuck does that mean?" Manny asked, cocking a bushy black eyebrow at pale little George. George pulled out his phone and checked the intraoffice schedule. He read today's entry: "Delivery and installation of BMW Authorized 55-inch Multitouch Screen Desktop Worktable with wireless interactive technology and iStick/Airscreen, with built in LED and Apple 40-inch tablet computer interface with disappearing screen option. Suggested user: Head of Finance."

At that moment, George and Manny heard knocking on the wall. A voice with a foreign accent yelled through the drywall: "I come heir von BMW Munich mit large computer glass Vorktable. Please mach schnell into toilet, Herr Smithson, mit der Freund Manny Nichols. I enter office im fumf minutes. Installation computer Vorktable is BMW 'essential business.' Quarantine? I see nuttin! I know nuttin!"

George's eyes were huge. He vaguely remembered a memo six months ago, after one of the big shots had visited from Munich and seen the state of Smithson's outdated office, and that this BMW big shot, Herr Reinhardt Zeitgeist, might be express-shipping a new desk for the finance office.

George is the kind of accountant that misses things when they have to go. He looked fondly down at the old Formica desk, worn away at the edges where his sleeves had rubbed for 15 years, and said to the German voice on the other side of the wall: "You mean Mr. Nichols and I are to go into my bathroom together while you install a new desk in here? We've got a problem, then, with that, I'm sorry to say! We're supposed to be in lockdown. The State has ordered us to be locked in place for six weeks. We'll be reported to Command!"

The German voice replied: "Ich bin a Deutsche citizen. Your American rules mean nuttin zu me. BMW is mein Commandant. Der BMW Authorized 55-inch Multitouch Screen Desktop Worktable ist superior to your American trash."

"Hell, Smithson," Manny said, "let's jump into the bathroom. Sounds like this desk might be well-engineered."

Thus, they found themselves in the bathroom—George perched on the toilet bowl, and Manny leaning against the door. George did not like to touch doors or door handles.

Manny and George heard the foam around the office door drop as it was dug out. They heard a whir of a power tool as it trimmed the adhesive from the frame. They heard the door open and the sound of booted feet marching into finance. They heard a big box being dragged into the office and opened, and they heard grunts appropriate to the lifting of heavy glass. They heard the German installer begin to build George a new desk.

Manny called to the German voice, who by the sound of things, was an engineer: "What's the model of that baby? What can she do? Any factory extras?" Remembering that it was German engineers who developed the lockdown foam sealant, Manny had great confidence in German engineering.

The voice, now feeling heard by a fellow gearhead, said: "Ja, das ist ein touchscreen glass computer table mit refrigerated cooler drawers for bier und wasser unter."

"You don't mean it's a console table using integrated hardware, do you? And it has a fridge?"

"Ja, Munich sagt it is perfect for interactive financial contract-building fur neu buyers at BMW, und ist die beste fur die 'compelling sales experience mit multi-touch plate glass screen ease of use'"—they heard grunting and swearing—"aber ist zu heavy, the son of a bitch." The German engineer said this with some difficulty, as he hefted up the 55-inch plate glass tabletop of the giant computerized workstation.

"Remember your fulcrum, you dumb Kraut!" Manny shouted, as he heard the serious grunts of heavy lifting through the bathroom door.

After about an hour of clanging and noisy electrical tools, the voice said, "Fertig. Alles Klar, alles Gut. Ich gehe. Auf Wiedersehen."

Manny and George exited the toilet and beheld a beautiful computer the size of a two-man desk, with no keyboard, no printer, no anything, just a sleek plate of glass, perched upon a desk-like cabinet that contained a small refrigeration unit for cold beer and soft drinks. Manny leapt to one side of the desk, divided by two opposing screens, and with a wave of his hand the computer jumped to life and spoke, thankfully in English, explaining what it could do. Manny listened with rapt attention.

A few hours later, at midnight, George and Manny were playing online bridge, separately. Their separate games were perhaps an apt metaphor for quarantine: a game of the art of being alone together.

George enabled the workstation's dual computer function, so that he could play with live people, while Manny learned to play against the computer. In a few minutes, on opposite sides of the desk, Manny was playing the International Bridge Association's automated gaming system, and George opted to play against three other live players of similar algorithmically assessed skill levels. George, deep in the game within the hour, knew he was going to love the next 41 days.

ELIZABETH STEWART

Chapter 10

Discovery in the Legal Sense

L egal conference tables are frequently host to confusion, particularly at Liederkranz, Campbell, Sheffield and Spray LLP, a firm that specializes in trusts and estates. If the firm's conference table could speak, it would tell tales of disinheritance, infidelity, donations of large sums of cash to humane shelters for dogs instead of sons and daughters, and behests of millions to pool boys and busty young secretaries.

Because they heard so much, the conference tables in Carol Liederkranz's law office were changed for newer, less-burdened tables every five years or so. Otherwise, the beleaguered conference tables could never have held the weight of the human problem of passing along generational wealth.

That was Carol's job, at which she had earned a reputation as a legal wunderkind. She employed her husband, Reedley, as a financial planner. He hadn't always been a financial planner, but under direction from Carol, he had, in 2008, chosen a vocation with less exposure to younger women. Thus Reedley, educated in theology, was forced to leave his calling and turn to managing other people's money.

Reedley had an eye for the younger ladies, and if he couldn't have them in person, he had planned to build one. She was going to be perfect. He spent sleepless nights building his dream woman.

When his Monitor Bracelet flashed red, red, red, a collection of people led by Dr. Leonard Funicle was seeking legal advice in Carol's office. Their monitors had also flashed red, locking them all in place. And moments before that, Reedley had come face to face with the creation that he had built in his bed over long hot weeks. She was Dr. Funicle's daughter, Amalie Mercedes Funicle, a naturally beautiful 20-something hippie girl.

Reedley had based his development of the perfect woman on the Mercedes Benz website, where he had built his wife's fancy new car in 2019, and ordered the car

"as built." Why not build a woman from the top down just like that? And so he did. And that day, sitting across from him at his wife's expensive and overburdened conference table, he found that make and model in the person of Amalie Mercedes Funicle.

Carol didn't miss much, either as a lawyer or as a very bright woman in her fifties. The problem for Reedley was that she knew about a little peccadillo of his, that he had a vivid imagination when it came to sex with women under 25. She had sensed the frisson in the air when he looked at Amalie and her natural hippie beauty. Carol noticed right before the State's truck began to seal the second-floor window of the firm's Washington brownstone.

Carol was locked in place with Reedley, Amalie, Amalie's young boy Robert, and Amalie's parents, Dr. and Mrs. Funicle. Amalie was the embodiment of Reedley's dream girl, whom he had built just for himself. It had taken him until his late middle age to create something this perfect just for him, and there she was.

And there was his wife, solid, steely, tall, and commanding, at the head of the second-floor conference table.

Dr. Funicle, locked down along with his wife, Mary, was full of angry dismay as he studied the faces around the four-year-old flecked marble conference table. He possessed the piercing gray eyes of a practiced orthopedic surgeon, used to wielding scalpels. Those eyes were fixed on the skinny and slightly balding Reedley, the cause of it all. Reedley had been shocked into loss of bladder control when he beheld Amalie, his dream girl, and he had peed on his feet. Reedley was using those pink feet to fish under the table for his uncomfortable pair of Oxfords. What an ass, thought Dr. Funicle. He fumed as only a rich surgeon can fume when a lesser man is fishing for his wet shoes with skinny, damp feet.

Carol's 25 years in trusts and estates had proven that she could handle a family gathering, no matter how contentious. She was consistently in charge of herself and of potentially argumentative situations. She had to think of an ice breaker, and quickly.

"Since we are in this quarantine together for six weeks, why don't we go around the table," Carol said. "Each person here will tell me a little about themselves. I'll make some espresso, and we can get acquainted."

Carol darted into the kitchenette for milk and delicate cookies and chocolates. Eight-year old Robert Ford Funicle, Amalie's son, who had never eaten tea cookies or Godiva chocolate on the farm, followed Carol into the kitchenette, as did Mrs. Funicle. Rewarded with treats by Carol, Robert stepped out of the kitchenette with a napkin full of Godiva patisserie truffles. Carol returned to the head of the conference table. Robert pulled a small rolling secretarial chair to the two-part corner window of the conference room. Cocking an ear, he heard machinery noise outside, and balanced on his knees to gain a vantage point. A large State truck with hoses was in the street below the window; the riggers began to foam-seal the frame of the window.

As the adults shifted uncomfortably in their Chippendale chairs, Robert peered out of the window, beyond the truck and the rig's busy crew. His attention was caught by the little Washington, D.C., pocket park beneath him. Trees! A vacant pair of swing sets! Empty tennis courts beyond! Deserted basketball courts! He wished he were out there to keep the park company.

Consoling himself with the mound of chocolate in his lap, he tuned out the nervous voices of the adults around the conference table, who had not noticed the room's only large set of windows, or Robert's position as look-out there. With great interest, he saw a quick darting movement around a tattered basketball hoop across the street. He watched a pair of squirrels chase each other. No kids, only squirrels? It isn't raining, he thought. Why weren't there any kids playing?

Carol was at the conference table waiting with a smile for Dr. Funicle to share his story. Carol had been working on his trust for two years, but she didn't know much about Dr. Funicle's tastes or pleasures. She had been all business, as his estate totaled six million dollars. Dr. Funicle, tall and severe, wore two pairs of glasses at once, one perched on the end of his nose and one on the top of his distinguished mane of gray hair. He was a man of science and disliked talk.

As Mrs. Funicle returned with coffee and treats, Dr. Funicle said, " don't feel much like sharing right now, Mrs. Liederkranz."

Mrs. Funicle was fussy and alert, a bird of a woman with too many pearls. Since she usually covered up for her husband when he was too abrupt, she volunteered to speak with an understanding smile.

"Counsel Liederkranz, I will speak for us both," Mary Funicle said. "As you see, I raised one beautiful child, Amalie, who is now 24. Because she was such a handful growing up, questioning everything, getting into fights, and challenging her teachers, I really never worked outside the home. I loved to cook, and to arrange flowers for the church. I saw my role as a support to my husband and home and daughter. When Amalie was 16, she had Robert, my grandson. I have tried to help raise him, but I hardly ever get the chance. They live out in the country. But I love my family!"

Mary Funicle walked to her grandson Robert at the window, reached her little bird claw hand over Robert's cheek, and tweaked.

Amalie rolled her big brown eyes with their distinctive areole of yellow around the pupil. "Robert, please come to the big table. We want to hear you talk to us," Robert's mother said.

Robert had serious green eyes, curly reddish hair that flowed down to his waist, a perfect complexion much used to sun and wind, and clothes that were not new or clean. Even though now he looked like a bear cub that had been dragged to civilization, in about 14 years he would rise to the top of the theater world with his perfect male beauty and sensitivity of expression in his face and body. But right then, he was a wild young child who was about to be locked down with five adults for 42 days.

Robert obliged his mother and spoke. "I like to be outside on the farm," he said. "Mom and I have chickens." None of the adults asked him why he loved his chickens or his farm. Robert returned to the window.

When Amalie spoke, her voice was indeed perfect. Reedley believed he had built her voice to praise him. She said, in a small and musically feminine voice, "We have about 40 acres in the back woods of Virginia, where I live with eight other woman farmers, who want nothing to do with corporate America. We all work together and raise chickens and grow cannabis while we help raise each other's kids. We homeschool, and we grow our own food. Our goal is to be self-sufficient and keep away from the law and the authorities. My fellow farmers would laugh if they saw me in this law firm waiting to talk about an inheritance. Some of us have been wanted by the law for illegal grows, so I know a little about the law. I know enough to avoid it. I only came in here today because my dad wanted me to."

As Reedley listened to Amalie, his face fell. Maybe Amalie liked women. Maybe she lived on a lesbian commune. He pictured Amalie kissing the ripe mouth of a nubile fellow twenty-something on the farm. That could be interesting as well, he thought. When they escaped out of there, and she took him to meet the girls, it could really be quite a party. He hoped they all looked like her. His imagination ran wild: he pictured eight beautiful hippie farmer-ettes rolling in Virginia cannabis with him.

Some men have little regard for reality when sex, especially kinky illicit outdoor sex, enters their imagination. Reedley's imagination got his ass kicked out of the Arlington pastorate after his Methodist Church's youth retreat in 2008. That landed him in financial management under the watchful eyes of his wife.

Amalie looked at Reedley. What a creep, she thought. She felt trapped by Reedley's gaze. But the practiced confidence in Carol's dark brown lawyer's eyes helped her think the quarantine might be bearable. On the other hand, she was dismayed by the anger in her father's eyes and the mist in her mother's. She pitied her wild young boy, about to be cooped up with all those adults, but she felt sorrier for herself. What would she do here, she thought, stuck in a law firm with her mom and dad and that creep?

She felt trapped just at the mention of the law. She had, after all, been a cannabis grower before such a crop was State-sanctioned. She disliked anything organized, or any hint of institutional rules, tradition, or systematic structure. She longed to be back at the farm. She loved the humid air and the stink of the chickens, and she loved a nice joint now and again. Anything to stop this talk at the conference table. She stood from her Chippendale and faced the full bookcases, with their weighty tomes of legal books, which lined three walls of the conference room.

She pulled down a big legal book in red, her favorite color. It was *The Redbook: A Manual on Legal Style* by Bryan A. Garner. Carol watched Amalie with some interest. Amalie would never understand the polished, adept legal mind of the author, thought Carol. Bryan Garner, Carol's hero, was a lexicologist, linguist, and lawyer. Way over this poor hippie-girl's tousled head. Carol smiled to herself.

Suddenly, having paged halfway through the book, Amalie turned to Carol. "Why does the law exist? Why do you learn to write for the law in a certain way? What is legal language for, exactly, and how does it differ from a serious conversation? What are people like you meant to do for humanity? What makes a lawyer a lawyer? Is the legal profession different from the law?"

As if to emphasize the formal legal conference room as the perfect scene for her questions, Amalie gestured around the traditionally appointed room with its impressive leather-bound tomes. She looked Carol straight in the eye, challenging Carol to answer back, and answer well.

Carol was taken aback. "I haven't thought about the law like that since law school,

Amalie," she said. "You ask what people like me are trained to do. Well, we are trained to practice the law, and the problem with 25 years of practice is that we forget the philosophy that interested us in the idea of the law originally. We two do have some time before us, and I hope I can tackle some of your insightful questions."

"Our family came here to listen to your presentation of my parents' trust as it regards Robert's college education in the future," Amalie continued, pushing at Carol. "Who thought of a trust? What is the tradition that says someone's money can be passed down for a certain reason, under certain predetermined conditions? On the farm we are against personal property in all forms. When did the law invent inheritance? Does the idea of an inheritance come from history?"

Carol was amazed. A hippie girl with a brilliant, incisive mind. If Carol were interviewing Amalie for Harvard Law School, her alma mater, she would be interested in this young woman.

Amalie, once she formed an argument, always pursued it. "I mean, why are we here in your office?" Amalie said. "I had asked my father why he wanted to pass anything on to me or Robert. Dad is hopeful that there will be a future, perhaps without grounds, and the law gives him a structure for that hope. With global warming and now this virus crisis in 2020, we might not be around. I suggested to Dad that if he wants to be that hopeful, he should pass his money to his great-grandchildren. Robert, I am sure, won't want money. He's been raised to hate all it stands for."

Carol smiled. This clever hippie was asking about the age-old legal rule against perpetuity, and she had it right. Carol was pleased. She might have someone to talk to, maybe someone to mentor, if she played her cards right, during 42 days of quarantine. Amalie reminded Carol of herself at that age. Amalie clearly was not afraid of Carol, or of any other authority figure in the room, such as her stern and wealthy father.

Carol, pleased to find a potential new friend in young Amalie, might have been shocked if she knew what her husband was feeling. Reedley was feeling both lust and horror. He was horrified that his own creation, the woman he had built from scratch, was voicing these argumentative questions that made his disciplined, brilliant wife smile. Amalie had been built with a perfect exterior. She should have had a dull, simple, fun, sexually aroused brain, in his book.

He had assumed that if he had designed the exterior to perfection a perfect mind would follow: a simple, sweet temperament. But he was in quarantine, locked in place for 42 days, with what appeared to be a smart woman. This quarantine might be the worst of all possible scenarios, because there were now two smart women in one small conference room. Smart women, like his wife, had caused him more effort than he cared to have in his 50-plus years.

Living with a smart female mind for 28 years will eventually castrate a man, he thought. He had had enough of a good female mind with Carol. When he built the woman who in his dreams resembled Amalie, he desired someone to love him. That was a one-way street. He did not desire someone he had to love or respect. Reedley, although he had been taught that love is love when given, not taken, had forgotten how to practice that kind of love, if he had ever learned it in the first place.

Forget a mind. He wanted a perfect female chassis. Reedley stared at his still-damp Oxfords, upon which he rested his skinny pink feet. Shit, he thought. What went wrong?

Amalie saw that Carol was internalizing her many legal questions, and Amalie saw the intelligence in Carol's eyes behind those glasses. Amalie smiled as Carol handed her a chocolate and an espresso. Carol gestured in welcome to the conference room sofa, and she and Amalie sat down together with their coffees over *The Redbook*.

Reedley watched in disbelief. This quarantine was going to be a meeting of two attractive people, and neither of those two people were Reedley. Worse, the two attractive people had exceptionally fine minds, and both were female. A little overheard conversation—Amalie's questions and Carol's answers—had proven that both minds had that ultra-annoying attention to detail in language. What a fucking mess, the crumbling of all his best-laid plans. What a fucking bummer, a smart woman in a perfect body.

Carol laughed with delight as Amalie whispered a question in her direction that reminded her of her own questions to her favorite law professor years before. "Is there anything absolute about the law?"

Carol laughed at the profundity of this question, saying, "Well..."

"Come on, I bet you can explain that better." Amalie clearly liked a little conflict, a little argument. She had a natural tendency to ask about meaning and question a lack of detail.

Goddamn it, Reedley thought. From the frying pan of Carol's mind during 28 years of marriage into this fire of a quarantine. He had landed in a quagmire of two good female brains. He knew he'd never last the 42 days. He'd sure had high hopes for that perfect body. All he wanted was appearance, not content. He was beginning to feel quite ill.

Carol looked hard at Amalie. "We will have some time where we will be forced to be together," she said. "What would you think if I could convince you that the law is interesting, that lawyers are annoying but challenging, and that the law might be exactly right for a mind that works as well as yours? What if we used some of our time locked in here to see what I can show you in these books? What if you could use your good mind in a certain established format, a style of thought? A little coaching, and we can explore a legal future for you, together." Carol leaned back on the sofa, smiling a warm smile. Amalie looked skeptical but warily interested.

Carol continued, "If you didn't look at me like you doubted me, I wouldn't be asking you these questions. I think you'd make a great lawyer."

Oh, for fuck's sake, thought Reedley. He'd worked for six months designing her, and what did he get? One more smart fucking woman who could turn every simple problem into an endless what-if situation. One more smart fucking woman who answered every simple, non-complicated, obvious-ass statement with "What do you really mean?" One more smart fucking woman to ask, "What does your choice of language say about your intentions? What do your words mean? What do they imply?" God, the sheer headache of it all.

Reedley's head was in his hands. He saw what the next 42 days would hold: pain for him, and sisterhood for two smart women. His entire project of building the perfect woman was up in smoke, now that he had found her. Poof. Except for her good mind, she'd be ideal.

It was his fault, he thought, sardonically. He had neglected to erase the important synapses that formed creative and intelligent thoughts in his dream woman's head, if such a synapse choice had been available on this imagined "build" site. He had hoped for his perfect woman to say extraordinarily little and giggle often. He didn't want a woman who must be right. He didn't want a female existential philosopher. He just wanted to get laid by a pretty young girl. Where did she go? Now all he saw was another Carol! He began to feel nauseated.

On the other side of the conference room, Carol drew closer to Amalie on the sofa, and said, "Now, Amalie, persuade me that you should not learn anything about the law." She smiled at the young hippie girl, who was reaching for Garner's *Guidelines for Drafting and Editing Contracts.* Carol formatted her question in the contrary for a reason. Anyone who has a lawyer in the family will know this tactic of reverse argumentation.

Amalie paged through Garner's book. Instead of answering Carol's question, she said, "What does it mean to make a contract?"

Reedley, who had peed his shoes over Amalie's natural beauty four hours before, ran for the conference room trash can. He was going to be sick.

123

124

Book III

The Big Reveal

The Gift of
Quarantine

Chapter 11

The (World-Famous) Forget Me Never Liquor

Forget Me Never! The liquor that made a lowly dive bar famous throughout the world was created through a progression of accidents. The first was the tragic accident of the pandemic, which lead to a 42-day forced quarantine in the Forget-Me-Not bar and the accidental assemblage of an odd assortment of folks.

The famous liquor was an accident of creative happenstance and gradual enlightenment of the seemingly washed-up Matt Early, who came to understand for the first time in his life that he couldn't occupy himself solely with drinking. Matt, locked in place with five hospitable, dissimilar strangers at the Forget-Me-Not, was learning how to divert his specific curse into a blessing, and learning to be an artist. The luckiest creative people work at their art, welcoming random accidents along the way. The accidents provide the creative mind with new inspiration; the work is up to the artist. Along the road of a 42-day quarantine, the company of five at the Forget-Me-Not discovered that creativity is the finest distillation of the spirit of life.

In their final days of lockdown at the Forget-Me-Not, the five coinhabitants encountered a monumental accident occasioned by the bar's long-time janitor and cook, Hymen. Sometimes a simple mistake leads to a great and fortuitous discovery, and the better part of this discovery is often self-discovery, and that is what happened at the Forget-Me-Not.

At the Forget-Me-Not Bar and Grill, Matt had stumbled upon a liquor recipe by experimenting with a distillation of cheap red wines and a blend of vanilla and some old chocolate powder. But the palate, the resonance, the taste of the liquor itself was far from perfect. The problem may have been the heat ratios, or perhaps the mix of ingredients, or maybe the problem was how to find the most flavorful mix of ingredients within the limited cache in the dive bar's kitchen. But Matt was not giving up; he continued to distill every day.

One evening, as the company gathered for their nightly tasting, Paco, exhibiting quarantine fatigue, said, "I don't feel like tasting your swill again, Matt. I am sketching a new motorcycle design. You'll never get the blend right, anyway."

"I'd like to bring you a glass, Paco," Matt replied. "I think I have it almost perfect." Matt then turned to Jasmine, who had just emerged from the basement of the bar, and also offered her a glass to taste. Her self-appointed project was to clean up 30 years of Emilio's junk. Over the years, Emilio had scavenged for old tools and machines thrown into the city garbage cans. Like most war babies, Emilio couldn't pass a broken piece of machinery without being tempted to give it a home.

Jasmine had worked hard and had amassed a pile of items to be tossed out as soon as they were out of quarantine. Emilio couldn't bear to see that pile, but he knew it was necessary. Jasmine had amassed a special small-machine parts stash, which she kept in a mop bucket that Matt had been using for the run-off of his distillation. She secretly dumped the smelly liquid out and filled the bucket with hunks of machinery parts that she wanted to show Paco. She collected the ones that were beautiful to her. Back in Haiti, she had also scavenged for machine parts, and had an eye for beauty in unlikely things. Tomorrow, she'd let Paco in on her secret stash, and show him what she had found.

Reaching out to Jasmine with a full glass, Matt now offered her a taste of his latest distillation batch. "Jasmine, here, have a nip," Matt said. "Tell me if you think it's is too heavy on the tannin. I tried to reduce it as best I can."

Jasmine drank, made a face, and said, "Matt, I wonder if you will ever be as good as the moonshiners in Haiti. When they can't get a batch right, they make a dance to welcome into the process our Baron Samedi, of the loa of our Vodou gods, The Baron, the master of all intoxications."

Emilio concurred. "In Italy, when we make our grappa, we invoke Bacchus, the trickster god of the drink."

Together, smiling at Matt, Jasmine and Emilio called out to Baron Samedi and Bacchus. "Come down!" they said. "Come down and help our friend Matt!" Matt smiled back. He could use some divine intervention if he was going to achieve the perfect blend. Jasmine winked at Matt and scooted back downstairs.

"Emilio, I know it's getting late," Matt said, "but perhaps the next batch, I'll add a little less vanilla, and cook the whole thing at a lower heat, for longer, and add a pinch more raw cocoa bean at the end. Or maybe we can vat-sit this batch with a little whole vanilla bean? What do you think?"

Emilio glanced at the Budweiser Clydesdale neon bar clock over the bar: Saturday at 11:45 p.m. "Matt, let's try that vat-sit idea of yours, this time with vanilla bean, overnight. Like the worm in the mescal, the vanilla bean in the Forget Me Never...why not? Let's get a hot pad to set 'er on to cool on the floor of the hot water heater closet in the kitchen. A little warmer environment might help. But we need to leave it uncovered to breathe. After a night, warmed a little, and breathing, we'll cook 'er again. We haven't tried that yet. And then let's all get some sleep."

Hymen lumbered in, rubbing his his eyes. He was the only one of the company at the Forget-Me-Not who had reversed his sleep schedule. Hymen slept during the day and came alive at night, to prepare treats for the five, and to clean the place. As a merchant marine sailor from Brazil, he had no trouble with curtailed sun to dark ratios, and enjoyed the peace and quiet of the deep wee hours when he could get some of his janitorial chores done around the bar.

You would think Hymen's job might have gotten easier since Emilio had no customers these days, but in fact, it was harder. Five people eating in the small restaurant kitchen, the short order stove with its big hood and grease trap, two bathrooms to clean, and five people bathing from sinks meant for washing hands. Hymen, who was mechanical, had rigged up an enlarged drain for both bathrooms so that water from spot bathing could drain on the old tiled floor.

Hymen was resourceful; he could make anything work with a few simple tools. He had lots of old pipes and tools and gears to choose from, unearthed from Emilio's basement, thanks to Jasmine. He puttered with the plumbing around the bar to make drinking water more available, and he engineered a system for five people to sleep with a modicum of privacy. He rigged flip-down style beds out of old bar tables, similar to the beds used by ship crews. Without Hymen, nothing about the practical life of quarantine would have gone as smoothly.

Hymen had a knack for invention, and he jerry-rigged the machinery and equipment needed for distilling the future elixir of the gods, Forget Me Never. He gathered old kettles, hoses, tubes, and nozzles that Emilio had saved over the years from behind the bar.

Hymen's greatest invention, Matt's main distillation vessel, was a stainless 24-quart tall-sided heavy pail, an ancient industrial mop bucket for which he had created a removeable assemblage of parts and pieces that accomplished, quite efficiently, a tight distillation system. Hymen had found a couple funnels and had welded them together to create a pressurized chamber. Various valve closures could be opened and shut on the makeshift distilling unit. It was like a stainless octopus built from scrap, but it worked. Hymen was proud of his contribution to the Forget Me Never distillation project of Matt's, and liked to spend his night hours tinkering at improving the distillation machinery. His pride and joy were the bucket's attachments, which were detachable from the bucket so that the mixture could cool and be reheated without transferring the liquid into a new distillation chamber.

Late that Saturday night, Hymen had awoken to his morning. He kept the bar and kitchen lights low, as the others were sleeping. And he had to be very quiet. For a man his size—he was six foot five and 320 pounds—he was virtually noiseless, and was able to see in the half-light. His years of training on a ship proved valuable.

Saturday night into Sunday morning was cleaning night, and Hymen had one area to focus on: the kitchen floor. The floors were sticky from the ongoing distilling project, and if Hymen didn't mop them vigorously each week, mold had a tendency to gather around the refrigerator vents near the floor. Hymen gathered up his mops, brooms, and scrub brushes to do a first-rate job on the kitchen floor.

Hymen had made a special disinfectant concoction, using some of the alcohol that Matt distilled off the ancient red wine. With the proof of the alcohol almost 40 percent, it could disinfect almost any floor. He had to conserve his special disinfectant, so he had claimed one of the two old stainless 24-quart buckets for his own. When Matt disliked a batch of his brew, Hymen claimed it and topped off his cleaning pail. He stored the bucket and its contents in a closet in the women's bathroom.

"Damn it," he said, in a whisper, "I can't find my mop bucket. Who would steal my mop bucket?" Hymen opened cabinets, checked under the sink, and checked the men's room closet. No mop bucket. Hymen looked at the barroom janitorial closet. Next, he checked the kitchen closet, which also housed the hot water heater.

He opened the hot water heater closet. "Oh, there you are!" Anxious to get started with his chores, he plunged his mop into the bucket he had found there, hiding in the dark, and commenced to mop the kitchen floor, re-dipping the mop after every 10 feet of floor. Every so often, to cut the disinfectant, he splashed the floor with a mixture of baking soda and water, another old seaman's trick for cleaning.

When he had finished, the floor smelled like a cocktail, but it gleamed in the half light. Almost 6:00 a.m., it was Hymen's bedtime. He closed the hot water closet door, leaving his bucket safe inside where he had found it.

Sunday morning, Matt awoke and hauled the cooled batch of Forget Me Never from the hot water heater closet, where he had left it to vat-sit overnight. He attached Hymen's elaborate hoses and valves into the removeable top, and re-seated the lid. Once the rig was sealed, he put it on the range to distill the mixture one more time. He hoped the vanilla bean in that gradually cooling chamber would improve the recipe. He watched as the distillation process began its alchemical progression on the range. An hour later, the most delicious smell wafted through the kitchen, so fine a smell of so fine a distilled liquor that it roused Emilio out of sleep.

Without stopping to pull on his shoes, Emilio came padding into the kitchen. "What have you created, Matt! I think you have finally done it! This stuff smells beautiful, bene, bene!" Matt smiled broadly and gave him a glass of the warm golden liquid to taste. Emilio tasted the concoction. "Not only is the odor one of perfection, indeed heavenly, but the taste! Nectar of the gods!"

Matt, tears in his eyes, embraced the old Italian, who was also tearing up. "You did it. You are a creator!" he said to Matt. And then in Italian, Emilio said, "Creatore! Enologo! Vinaio! Artefice!"

Jasmine, meanwhile, had woken Paco at 7:30 a.m. from his slumber on the red vinyl banquette, and had led him down to the basement to show him the machine parts she had specially selected.

"Grab your sketchbook, Paco," she said. "You can make sketches of these pieces so that when we're out of here, you can find out what they are."

With Jasmine's help, Paco sorted through a few of the broken pieces of old motors, gaskets, cams, crankcases, and he began to see that he was examining pieces of an old motorcycle, specifically a kind of old bike called a Board Track Racer. Those bikes were legends!

"Where did you find these parts?" he asked Jasmine, as he pulled them out of an ancient stainless mop bucket.

133

"Most of those small ones? From that old boy's bike in the corner," she replied. In the dim basement light, Paco could make out a fabulous machine.

No ordinary bike, this was a two-wheeled machine that had cylinder barrels, and Paco could see that they had been deeply spigoted into the crankcase, and that the combustion chamber seemed to be a hemi with exhaust valves set at an unusual 70 degrees to each other. Paco, who was passionate about motorcycles, knew he was looking at something he would never forget.

Overcome, Paco grabbed Jasmine and gave her a big hug. "I'm sure I am looking at the OHC V-twin, something from maybe my grandpa's day. It's broken up, but it's a beauty. I'll never forget this, Jasmine. This bike will never leave my imagination, and neither will you, as you look to me right this minute." A little abashed, they sat down together on an old crate. Paco sketched the shape of the pistons so he could later create a prototype of their original innovative shape.

Paco worked on his sketches all day Sunday. He produced, amongst other wonderful drawings of the bike and its pieces, a glorious drawing of the Board Track Racer's most iconic piece of machinery: the shaft and bevel drive single overhead cams with pistons. Some of his drawings featured the bright cheerful face of Jasmine, some focused on her hands holding the handlebars of the old Racer, and some sketches revisited the image of Jasmine in the half-light holding an ancient stainless bucket filled with machine pieces.

Meanwhile, in the bar kitchen, Emilio looked deeply into the vat of the nectar of the gods, Bacchus' gift, and studied the newly created vat of sweet-smelling liquor. The color was not what Emilio expected. Emilio saw a dark caramel brown with a silt of white powder around the edge of the bucket. Previous distillations had been almost colorless.

He couldn't contain his curiosity. Emilio shook the sleeping form of the huge man till he awoke. "Hymen, did you leave your mop bucket in the kitchen closet last night?"

"Yessir!" said Hymen, "I was surprised to find it there." He told Emilio about the formula of his special disinfectant and baking soda that he used to kill the mold from the refrigerator vent.

"Mold. That's it!" Emilio remembered that mold had been the secret ingredient in his family's grappa. The combination of the triply distilled alcohol, the vanilla bean, the previous night's pinch of chocolate powder, a little of Hymen's baking soda—and, of course, the refrigerator mold—had resulted in a delicious aperitif-style liquor.

Hymen's mop was the catalyst and the accidental brew's secret magic wand. Hymen's mistaken bucket was the final blessed string in a series of accidents that had created this ambrosia of the gods. Accidents, Emilio remembered, are a favorite ploy of Bacchus, the trickster god, who plays with humans and leads them astray so that they can find themselves.

Today, Forget Me Never Inc. has bottled millions of liters of the delicious liquor, and has made Emilio, Hymen, and Matt millionaires five times over.

The labels on Forget Me Never feature a much-copied drawing of shaft and bevel drive single overhead cams, and the pistons that frame them, created by the famous artist Paco Picada. Those unique and unforgettable cams and pistons came from a 1915 Cyclone Track Racer (and by the way, a bike of this year and model was in the collection of Steve McQueen, the King of Cool). For the liquor's label, the pistons are boldly worked into the name of the liquor on the bottle, Forget Me Never, and the v-shaped pistons are below the "v" in Never.

Paco became well known for his edgy renderings of intricate iconic machinery that he worked into his highly sought-after paintings. And he became a beloved supporter of young, emerging artists from his wife's home country of Haiti.

And that is why, many years later, after Emilio retired to his beloved Sicily at the age of 90, Jasmine and Paco purchased the building in which the Forget-Me-Not was formerly located, and opened a world-famous gallery, which has given the world many talented artists who feed the spirit. They named that gallery Never Forget Love.

ELIZABETH STEWART

137

Chapter 12

Bombay's Brown Perfection Finds Home

Looking out the bay window of the Pin around 5 p.m. on the fifth Thursday of quarantine, Nancy Jean saw a small animal crate. What the hell, she thought, this is really too much. What kind of fool leaves a small animal on a doorstep during a 42-day quarantine? She saw, with dismay, a bag next to the crate with cans of cat food and a bag of kitty litter. A sudden rearrangement, a small upheaval that discloses the world's imposed disorder, was too much for Nancy Jean. An alteration to her expectation of order made her mad.

"I hate cats!" she spat out. "Elaine! Look at this. Some idiot thinks we need a cat. Whoever it was, he delivered the whole cat set-up!" Elaine put down her salon hairbrush (Nancy Jean had just finished Elaine's color for the day, another conservative sensible shade of The Perfect Brown, of course), and joined Nancy Jean at the window.

A furry black face with shiny copper-colored eyes peered out of the crate. "That's my Silky Boy!" Elaine squealed with joy.

Hearing this delighted squeal, Nancy Jean's long-time beauty operator, Denise Bustamante, awoke at the first sound of joy she had heard at the Pin in eight years. She had slept, stretched out in the janitor's closet of the Pin, through almost five weeks of quarantine, happily waking only to eat in solitude. What a relief to be away from her five kids, but five weeks of relaxation was getting old. She watched, drowsily, as Elaine pulled at the salon's front door in frustration, but it had been well sealed with foam.

With tears in her eyes from the effort, Elaine said, "Nancy Jean, it's Silky Boy! Can we bring him in! Bernard must have dropped him off!" Elaine continued tugging at the heavy plate glass door etched with the moniker "The Golden Pin-Up." The door was immovable. Faintly, the women could hear the plaintive mew of the cat. Denise watched carefully. She remembered something about a concealed door under the newer siding at the back of the salon, with its ancient opening directly from the interior of the color room.

Years ago, Nancy Jean had installed the secret exit door at the back of the salon, a false front to a wall hidden in the color room that opened to the alley. It had originally been used for ventilation in the days when blonde meant toxic bleach, but had gone unused for years. Nancy Jean rushed to the cash drawer where she thought she had hidden the key to the hidden door. Thank goodness, there it was, under a bowl of pennies. She slipped out the secret door, darted through the alley, and hefted the crate, food, and litter into the shop. Denise, meanwhile, sensing her golden opportunity, slipped out the secret door and headed down the marginally safe Topeka street for home. No one noticed.

"Here, take this thing," Nancy Jean said to Elaine, handing her the plastic crate with the wire door. Elaine sprung the door open, and cat and owner were united as Elaine lifted him to her heart. Silky Boy purred, low and long, and arched into Elaine's chest. Nancy Jean, a decided cat hater (she was a dog person), couldn't help but feel a twinge of emotion.

"I could stay here forever now that I have my boy!" said Elaine with an uncharacteristic show of emotion. "You know, Nancy Jean, these three weeks have been the happiest of my life. We have found formulas for the Perfect Brown together, and our meals are catered, and Bernard's far away, and now I am complete because Silky Boy has made us a perfect family!"

Previously, family had consisted of Elaine and her cat. Not until working with Nancy Jean on The Perfect Brown had Elaine realized that the family you are born into, or marry into, may not be the one you need. Elaine hadn't had children after the false pregnancy that ended in a meager marriage to Bernard. Nancy Jean hadn't known traditional family life either. Nancy Jean's husband, who was much older and had retired to his BarcaLounger, had sired a horrible set of twins 36 years ago, a product of a previous marriage, and hadn't wanted more.

141

Nancy Jean's eyes opened wide. "Well, I never knew you felt that way about family, Elaine, and yes, we are now fast friends. To be a family? Well, it must mean that you make a difference in the lives of those you love. It has been fun, this lockdown. No clients, no constant telephone calls, no appointments, no husband, and I have hours to experiment with our elusive shade of brown. But I should tell you, I am not a cat fancier. In fact, I am slightly allergic to cats." She could feel her sinuses constricting. "We might have to ask your husband to take him back if my nose acts up."

"Oh no, Nancy Jean, this cat makes everything even more perfect. Please, let us try for a few days and see if you can bear him. Once he gets to know you, he will win you over." As if on cue, Silky Boy mewed and wrapped his eight pounds of sleek black fur around the ankles and calves of doubtful Nancy Jean.

"He's a talker!" said Nancy Jean.

"Yes, and a lover, too. You'll see, you'll fall in love." Elaine lifted him again into her arms, holding him under the sleek shoulders and letting that long elegant body dangle in front of her. "Look at this perfect black coat!" Nancy Jean had to admit that the cat was gorgeous, with his deep black fur underscored with a rich perfectly warm purple-brown.

"Well, Silky Boy, you have put on weight! Look at that tummy! Bernard's been indulgent with you! We will have to diet, won't we, Boy?" said Elaine, thinking of Bernard's greasy packaged fish-sticks, most likely fed to the Boy while Elaine was out of reach.

Without looking to Nancy Jean for permission, Elaine allowed the Boy to roam through the salon. Silky Boy surveyed his new home.

Nancy Jean's brows tightened. Who does that cat think he is, a jungle panther? This was her jungle! Nancy Jean's strong will was showing, but Elaine was too delighted by the cat's antics to notice.

The salon was a cat's paradise. He found trash cans of ready-made hairballs, he found little silver clips that scuttled when he batted at them. He leapt on the chairs and slid on the vinyl seats. He jumped straight up onto the little ledges for hair products and smelled each bottle. He took drinks of water at three different sinks. He perched like a pasha on the porn-purple front desk. Nancy Jean had to admit he looked quite a picture with his sleek blackness on that shade of purple. He indeed looked like a little black panther; he had something wild about him but was as self-contained as a high-born gentleman. The cat seemed to smile.

Dinner for the ladies was slid in on a tray at the window cracked open five inches for just this purpose: filets of sole, rice pilaf, and a nice chardonnay. Silky Boy's pink nose was aquiver. Fish! The alpha cat in the Boy began to assert itself. Silky Boy yowled.

The table was laid, the wine was opened, two glasses were poured, and the two women sat down for their evening meal. Silky Boy, finding that yowling for a piece of fish got him no fish at all, posed beautifully on Nancy Jean's lap, unafraid of this rigid stranger when faced with the thought of a bite of fish on a plate. Nancy Jean ran her long fingers down his flexible spine.

Trying not to sneeze, she thought wine might help the allergies. She took a hefty swig. This cat seemed like a self-reliant, self-sufficient animal, she thought. Independent and orderly, qualities Nancy Jean respected. She had raised many little Jack Russell terriers, and this cat seemed to lower her heartrate rather than raise it, as in the case of the Jack Russells, which are veritable balls of energy. And dogs were so dependent on a person. Maybe she could get used to this cat. In fact, the compact, tall, and sinewy black cat in her lap resembled the tall, sinewy, straight-backed Nancy Jean, in more ways than one.

Dinner featured stories about Silky Boy's breeding. Elaine explained that he was a rare cat breed, a Bombay, which she had sought out because she had seen one at the International Cat Association Show six months ago. She had contacted the Bombay and

Asian Cats Breed Club for a list of breeders. Finding one in the Midwest, she had made Bernard drive her 150 miles to Chicago to purchase Silky Boy. He cost fifteen hundred dollars, the most money she had ever spent on anything. Not all that happy in her marriage, with Bernard being so disorganized, unfettered, and devoted to his social causes, Silky Boy was her baby. She became what you might call a "cat lady."

"The Bombay is not an old breed, and was recognized only in 1978," Elaine explained. "A cat breeder in Louisville, Kentucky, named Nikki Horner, crossbred her Grand Champion Sable Burmese with a black American Shorthair. The Shorthair had copper eyes. That was in 1953, the first of the breed."

For a shy, straight-laced lady, Elaine was anxious to talk about the details of breeding these rare cats, and she continued with more information than Nancy Jean needed at dinner. Still, Nancy Jean had to smile at her new friend's excitement and feline fascination. Talking well into the ten o'clock hour, both women retired to separate sides of the narrow salon and fluffed up their pillows.

Elaine asked Nancy Jean if she might have a drawer from the desk to make a bed for the Boy, and she lined it with many soft pink hand towels. The Boy, beautiful and content (he had managed to beg a piece of fish from Nancy Jean at dinner), kneaded the towels in the drawer's interior and cuddled down to sleep.

The new day dawned bright and peaceful, and the sound of the cat's purr alternated with the lapping of its sandpaper tongue. Something was different about the Boy's small noises this morning, thought Elaine, who had owned him for almost four months now. Donning one of the salon's maroon kimonos, Elaine walked to the Boy's drawer-bed. The Boy was softly licking five tiny wet-looking black kittens with tiny pink noses and tiny pink paws.

Silky Boy? Not a Boy? Someone must have let the cat roam. Silky Boy was Silky Girl. And now before her, Elaine saw six cats! All her strict ideas about what should be and what should happen and how surprises lead to chaos and disorder crashed down upon Elaine, and her eyes filled with soft tears. As she bent to look closer at the tiny perfect bodies, she felt Nancy Jean lean over her.

"Oh look, a new mother!" Nancy Jean smiled. She felt for Elaine's hand and squeezed it tightly. "You must be thrilled, loving these animals as you do. This is why Bernard dropped Silky Girl here. He must have known."

Elaine smiled, rolling her eyes. "Yes, Bernard is not one to face a challenge. What can you do? Men!"

Nancy Jean agreed. "My husband would have run the other way as well. Looks like we women face life on a different and higher level." Their hands still together, Nancy Jean gave Elaine a hug. "We will make sure these little ones are comfortable, and when we get out of quarantine, we will find them great homes. We can do this together!" All the years of disliking the straight, prim Elaine D. Jones, who was always prompt for her appointments and who sat so rigidly, holding her handbag on her lap, flashed in front of Nancy Jean's eyes. This sudden change in Silky Boy had caused a loosening of the laces around Elaine.

Two people who are very similar in temperament typically do not like each other. This is because we see what we dislike in ourselves in someone else, and we recognize—but do not admit—what we dislike in ourselves. In truth, we dislike a reflection of our own nature, and therefore we abhor the person who shows us this nature.

An event that softens the heart and reveals the advantages of flexibility helps us begin to appreciate that we can, indeed, recognize ourselves in another. And when we begin to see what is good in them, we see what is good in us.

Before their quarantine, they had been more alike than they knew. Now, after witnessing what they thought was a male cat give birth, could both women, not young anymore, let go of their old rigid ways of reacting to change? Life comes at us in surprises that lay beneath appearances. That was the lesson of the Bombay Boy who became a mother overnight.

When Nancy Jean saw that the Boy had given birth to kittens, she realized that to thrive one has to remain flexible within change, and she began at that moment to appreciate unpredictable life in its many changes. Nancy Jean also began to discover that she could bend, accept the inevitable, and welcome newness. In the year to come, Nancy Jean would begin to "let her hair down," to use a salon metaphor, and Elaine would soon follow suit.

About six months after quarantine was lifted at the Golden Pin-Up, Nancy Jean sold the beauty salon, and bought a 20-acre ranch in Montana with a 1920s craftsman-style two-story house. It was perfect for two women who liked peace and solitude and cats. Nancy Jean designed and paid for comfortable homes for 20 Bombay cats and kittens, with outbuildings for breeding and playing. Nancy Jean Hammily and Elaine D. Jones were soon considered the top breeders of Bombay and Asian cats in the country.

Their precision, their attention to detail, their fastidious natures, made them fine breeders, and perfect companions for each other, because they had a common goal that demanded precision. Bernard came to visit twice a year as a friend of the couple, but Mr. Hammily never came even though he was invited for Christmas.

At the Montana ranch, appropriately named Bombay's Brown Perfection, both women, in their late 60s, wore their hair in chemically different but nevertheless perfect shades of brown they invented while locked in place. Both browns were soft and age-appropriate, their own perfect formula for each other, and, indeed, a Perfect Brown that represented a blending of two similar natures and inclinations toward the new structure of their shared lives. The discovery of mutual love and respect happened sometime during 42 days of quarantine in the little color-mixing room at the Golden Pin-Up, and convinced two intractable souls that life is meant to be shared, and is meant to move us, as we age, into becoming more, rather than less, flexible.

Chapter 13

From the Horsewoman's Mouth

rs. Marion Folger had a heavy cannonball-sized Italian glass paperweight balanced in her large, meaty palm, and it's safe to say she was a pretty good shot. She was about five foot nine and 190 pounds, with an ample set of strong shoulders and a firm and shelf-like bustline. Her solid buttocks and thighs led to what some unkind men refer to as cankles, cylindrical lower legs straight down to the feet.

Having been trained by the best in the dental receptionist training department of the Kansas City Community College in 1973, Mrs. Folger wore what was *de rigeur* in those days. She was clad in a nurse's white lace-up rubber-soled shoes, a heavily starched and oft-pressed nurse's white dress uniform, a peaked nurse's cap, and professional white hose that emphasized her cankles. Because of her bulk, Mrs. Folger could have been mistaken for a large late-middle-aged man dressed like a female nurse.

Marion Folger was a white mountain of health and professionalism. At 65 years of age she had nary a gray strand in her short jet-black coiffeur, which she had set into a flip by a Kansas City stylist who hadn't changed her approach to hairstyling for 40 years. For 40 years, Mr. Folger had put up with a bedtime bonnet on his partner's head, though he never mentioned it. The bonnet kept Marion's flip in its gravity-defying outward curve. Final Net in the morning helped, too.

As Mrs. Folger guarded Elisa Morgantown with that cannonball of a paperweight, the contrast between the two women could not have been more marked. Elisa had lovely legs in threadbare knee-less jeans, showcased when she lay supine in the six-thousand-dollar Ritter dental chair. She also had a flat stomach. An admiring man might have said to a friend, "Buddy, such a sight! I could have bounced nickels off of it."

Elisa was slim and strong, five foot six and 120 pounds, and in her early 30s. She excelled in show jumping, dressage and three-day eventing, and her complexion spoke of moist horse barns and midwestern sunshine. She had no artifice, just an elegance that comes when a woman is good at a sport. Mrs. Folger suspected that Elisa might be short on intellect, but Ms. Morgartown had in her short life achieved a physical connection with the outside world that gave her acute powers of observation, and she remembered every detail.

There is a difference between intellect and intelligence, and Ms. Morgantown had intelligence, but little intellect, as demonstrated by her lack of understanding of the chicken joke. However, she had staying power, the kind that comes from hard work in the ring. She and her favorite Dutch Warmblood jumper, Alistair Ben, had won the Kansas State Fair Gold Medal in 2018 for individual and team eventing. Ms. Morgantown noticed things, and if something interested her, she could concentrate. Lest she be called dumb, keep in mind that intelligence can be kinetic. Kinetic people notice things and make good tellers of tall tales.

Unsurprisingly, given her figure, Mrs. Folger was also raised on a farm, outside of White Bear in Minnesota. Before meeting Bob Folger, Marion Wattala worked with her parents and six siblings on a 30-acre spread called 8 Roots, named by her poetess mother after the eight members of the family. The farm was down a short tree-lined lane in Grant, an unincorporated area of White Bear. You could smell White Bear Lake from the front porch.

Mr. Wattala was an old-school Polish-American farmer, but Mrs. Sybil Wattala was a poetess and novelist, and she had a few moderate sellers to her name. Because she grew up working the farm by day and reading with her mom in the evenings, Mrs. Folger loved to read. When inspired, her mom would say to Marion, "Take out your dictation pad. I feel a great story coming on!" Marion loved those evenings.

Mrs. Folger felt protective when she smelled the clean aroma of hay and manure still lingering on Ms. Morgantown's boots. At that crucial moment, cannonball paperweight in hand, Mrs. Folger said to Dr. Randolph Edwards, DDS, "Before I put this weapon back on your desk, Doctor, I am going to set the geographical limitations of this 42-day quarantine. Ms. Morgantown and I will spend the 42 days of quarantine in the waiting room. And you will spend the 42 days in this office of yours. When we need to speak to each other, we will do so in the operatory. At no point in the 42 days are you to be alone with Ms. Morgantown. Do I make myself clear?"

How could he disagree with a woman of Mrs. Folger's size and ferocity when she was holding a skull-shatterer? Dr. Edwards nodded his head in agreement. Ms. Morgantown, who understood the need for firmness with stallions, grinned.

Mrs. Folger and Ms. Morgantown established their separate sides of the Dental Arts office waiting room, which, like Dr. Edwards's office, had been designed by Dr. Edwards's efficient, multitasking wife, Trisk. It had a lively and colorful mural, painted by Trisk herself, depicting the agriculture of Kansas City, Kansas, in the 1850s. The style of the mural was Art Deco Social Realism, after the famous WPA murals on the walls of Kansas City municipal buildings.

The furniture kept the tone of the Art Deco period, with big, squarish, leather easy chairs, tiered glass end tables, and a pair of compatible Deco down-filled sofas. An up-light, hidden in the bright blue geometric Deco carpet, shone on a particularly virile bearded farmer, lovingly painted in Trisk's mural. The farmer was modeled on Trisk's great-great-grandfather, a Mennonite wheat farmer from Russia named Hiebert Giesbrecht. He had farmed land outside of Kansas City in 1854, when Kansas was opened for settlement.

Ms. Morgantown had seen this mural on the front page of Dr. Edwards's website. It was the reason she had selected Dr. Edwards's office for her dental care and put up with Dr. Edwards's clumsy flirting for five years. Ms. Morgantown loved everything about the mural, especially the story it told. Mrs. Folger loved it too. It was natural for Mrs. Folger to select the waiting room for their private sanctuary.

"That's Dr. Edwards's wife's ancestor, there, the one with the long beard furrowing the field," said Mrs. Folger. "Russian Mennonites coming to Kansas brought seeds of crops they had planted in their homelands. Mennonite settlers brought wheat, accustomed as they were to growing wheat in a prairie climate."

Ms. Morgantown studied the 20-foot mural again. She was fascinated with the connection to Dr. Edwards's wife's personal history. What a wonderful thing to be a creative person who could tell a story with pictures, Elisa thought.

"Do you think you could write a history of your family farm?" Elisa asked Marion, with whom she was now on a first-name basis.

"Well, I wish I could, and writing runs in the family, but I am a reader, not a writer. I took down the storylines for all my mother's novels though. What about you, Elisa, could you write or paint a family history of your farm?"

Elisa's family farm was Morgan's Castle, located between Tonganoxie and Kansas City, down a long country road in Basehor, Kansas. "Yes, I could tell you how wonderful it is, Marion. I can show you with word-pictures. But I don't think I could paint it. I never liked sitting at a computer to write, but I can tell stories!" She giggled.

Marion, efficient and practical, and acting from long-learned instinct, took a pad and pencil from her skirt's side pocket. Something about Elisa recalled Marion's novelist mother, and inspired Marion to take dictation. And she was right Although Elisa lacked a copious intellect, she noticed things, and that gift for noticing things about the life around her was her brand of intelligence. Elisa immediately noticed, and then remembered, objects, situations, and people, not to mention animals, shapes, movements, and personalities.

Elisa's eyes had a faraway look as she said, "To get to Morgan's Castle, you drive through a prairie landscape, hot in summer, and cold in winter. But if you come in the spring, ah! Spring is the time to visit our farm! 158th Street is verdant, and tree-lined because my grandfather planted maples, cool and green. You'll drive under them when you come in April. First, you'll see the paddock and our well-painted fences, kept fresh by Mr. Hobbs, our old farmhand, with us now for 34 years. Beyond the paddock stands the sturdy dairy barn, harboring a two-week-old calf, and two donkeys, who are sisters. Further in the barn, you'll smell first and then meet our friendly herd of Nigerian goats. You can taste the cheese we make, after our tour." Elisa smiled at Marion. "Can you see our Morgan's Castle?"

Marion replied, "Oh yes, I can. Keep going, it's lovely!"

Elisa continued, "Beyond the barn, clusters of cows nap and graze in the tall grass. There's my brother, with the green John Deere cap. He is attending Cal Poly for ag, but nature taught him first. He experimented with apples as a little boy. He is responsible for our apple orchard. Our little sister, Star, and her boyfriend, Jimmy, tend the chickens. Beyond the beehives, you can see the beekeeper's shack, bright white in the April afternoon sun. And look, there, at the stables, clad in flannel, with his easy way with the horses, is my father, David Morgantown, founder of Morgan's Castle. My dad is a respected breeder. He bred my horse, Alistair Ben, and other great Dutch Warmbloods. He chooses to breed the 'Bloods,' as he calls them, for their quality and performance as jumpers, not for their bloodlines. Because of dad, I studied jumpers, people, and movement all my life. He taught me to notice things."

Marion prompted her to continue. "We're going to write a book together, Elisa. Keep talking."

Elisa went on. "David Morgantown says that he likes a Blood to be 'built uphill,' which is a way breeders talk about the conformation of a natural jumper. A natural jumper is a horse that leans forward into a stride. Like most excellent breeders, my dad breeds for long necks and strong legs. He calls me his best mare for that reason."

Marion was right; Elisa Morgantown was a natural storyteller. Her words were

154

so rich, so descriptive, so detailed, and so visually evocative that Marion could see and feel her story as she told it. Before a writer can tell a story, a writer must have the courage to feel the story.

Elisa went on to tell more stories during the 42 days, all told to the patient and prescient Mrs. Folger. She told stories imagined from her life. Each of her characters were a little sliver from her own well-observed life. She learned that when time and space shrink, as they did during quarantine, imagination expands. Marion wrote those stories down for Elisa, as she had for her novelist mother.

Once Elisa was freed from the lockdown at the Dental Arts office, she began to write stories. In the year to come, she gained more confidence as a storyteller. She is writing her fourth book at this moment—this book. Your narrator is that woman, originally christened Elizabeth, and nick-named Elisa, who was quarantined in a dentist's office for 42 days, where she first discovered her art.

Chapter 14

The Dealership: Playing Cards

At midnight on the 30th day of quarantine, Manny had played over 50 boards of bridge on the newly installed BMW Worktable computer in George Smithson's finance office. George's analysis of Manny's plays became a favorite pastime for the ambitious Manny. George often asked Manny to explain hands from the beginning of play.

"George," said Manny, "on a three club, my bid, I was South, at simultaneous pairs, South, see? Board nine I played six of clubs, lead was ace of hearts. (Yes, you guessed it George, I am out of hearts.) All of a sudden, here comes West! And West was really good, a top player. East played the ace, I trumped it. Hell. What do you say, Georgie boy? I think I finessed!

George smiled his straight line of a smile with no teeth observable in Manny's direction.

"George! Tell me if I played this hand right." Manny was learning fast. George, who knew the game from his early years of playing the automated system at IBA, was a tremendous resource to Manny.

George patiently listened as Manny continued. "I think I finessed, George, can you believe it! Here's what happened: North/South won the contract at three clubs. Clubs are trump, which is a given. South is playing the hand and North is the dummy. Which meant that the dummy hand was revealed for all to see and the dummy just sat at the table and collected tricks as they were won."

George smiled. "Manny, I see. Some South players ask the dummy to pull the card they want to play rather than reach over, but the dummy can never say anything or choose a card on their own. So now let's say I have lots of clubs with my trump bid but I don't have the king. I play something to 'finesse' the king from the opposing hand during a non-trump trick. The reason being they will take the trick for sure, but they won't get two of my trumps in the process."

158

Manny, who took notes on his automated plays to discuss with George, stopped in mid-conversation, brows knitted. If depth of thought could create a personal steam cloud, George would have noticed steam rising from Manny at that beautiful workstation in the Sterling BMW finance office.

Manny, glaring at George in consternation, said, "George, listen to this. Trick four, my dreaded trick four. I led six of spades, but West, the sonofabitch (ok, I was playing the computer, but if West was a real guy, he would have been a turd), West goes with nine of clubs. That means West is trumping it with the nine. We lost the trick. I bit my nails; I'm counting cards, and sweating. I didn't want to lead trumps with my own hand! What do you think I could have led with instead of a spade? Because something went wrong."

George replied, "First I congratulate you, Manny, on your use of the necessary trump reduction. That trump reduction was a good move on your part, Manny, because you took one trump out of play."

"But we lost the trick!" said Manny. "How could that have been a good move?"

"You're going to lose tricks, George explained, "and that's one of the hard knocks of the game. Let's review a few foundational bridge truisms, however."

George leaned back in his chair at the workstation across from Manny. Manny's eyes were focused intently on George, both his hands flat on the glass table. "Manny, as the bidding unfolds, the communication goes forward. That communication is the language of bridge. The player who mentions a suit first is the one who plays it, if he wins the contract. But never forget the most basic lesson. You must follow suit if you have any of the same in your hand. In fact, the computer will stop you if you don't follow suit when you can."

"Wait a minute, George, what did you just say? The automated system will stop a player if a player doesn't follow suit when they can? Something stinks. Check this out, Georgie boy, in trick number four, when West trumped me on a spade trick, West subsequently played a spade in trick number six. I remembered thinking back to my dreaded trick four; when West trumped me, that meant he was out of spades, right? And then in six, by some miracle, or maybe by some computer glitch, West played a spade! IBA's automated system continued the game, and that's not the first time I noticed that happening."

Manny continued, "If what you say is true, that the system should catch a player when he doesn't follow suit, then I suspect a flaw in a system. I'm looking at my notes: out of my 50 boards played, the system failed to catch suit issues like the one I described to you 15 times!"

George smiled a wry smile, and said, "Manny, looks like you're onto something. I'm going to look into the automated system, because if what you say actually happened, there's something not quite right with the program; it didn't catch the basic suit rule. As I said, the computer should stop a player if you don't follow suit when you can. If you throw a legal card that wasn't the best card to throw, you're just a bad player, but if it's legal, the automated system will let you do it. If there's something wrong with the program, it might appear someone has cheated."

How did George know to follow his suspicion? Numbers people have intuition, and George's intuition was telling him something was wrong with the software of the International Bridge Association's automated online gaming site. The odds told him that Manny was right. George had heard Manny recite his losses for 30 days on 50 boards of bridge. Something didn't smell right. George saw numbers in certain colors and with certain smells, the unique gift of synesthesia in which one of the senses is simultaneously perceived as if by additional senses. Numbers for George were not just numbers, but sensory perceptions of smell and color.

George looked at Manny's tracking for his automated play, numbers meticulously kept by Manny the engineer. George suspected there was a flaw in the computation of the NeXtgen program on the IBA's online club site. Something wasn't working. Yes, this was a high-level established mathematical statistics program. But George Smithson was a CPA, and was so gifted with numbers he could smell a bad one.

Sure, there were 8,000 online members and 500 to 1,000 players online at any given moment. And lots of history to this venerable club site, too. It had its origins in the dark ages of online bridge; it was founded in 1994 by British mathematician Klaus Righteous. Some things about the site were superb. But if the automated program was flawless, a player must follow suit. Playing live, a player could make a mistake, or even cheat, and not follow suit, but he'd be called out, because everyone at the table would be counting cards and the other players make it their business to know what's been played and what cards are outstanding. To "follow suit" is at the core of bridge.

IBA had a great robot detection system, George knew that, and so the automated system was not all bad. George just knew there was something clunky and wrong about the NeXtgen program, overall. For example, it seemed too easy to understand how the program computed a player's expected average score so that suitable partners be found. This system should appear proactively inscrutable for fairness sake. He was going to crack the bug in the automated system, just like Manny was going to crack trump reduction. They had 15 days to work on their respective logic problems.

The processing power and computational ability of the new glass workstation in George Smithson's finance office at Sterling BMW was beyond excellent. Manny played bridge during the day and George worked on IBA's automated system problems during the nights. Both men were occupied in logic problems, stats problems, odds problems. Neither man missed the outside world in the least.

The IBA had a working management staff for the online club. Manny had played with a few staff members who had special bridge award names after their game handles, and George initiated correspondence with the IBA programmer-in-chief, Klaus Righteous. The founder also played but was getting on in years, and his game showed it. George suspected his programming skills were becoming rusty as well.

So George communicated via email with statistics and software staff member Tracy Kettering at IBA. George's emails proposed solutions to problems, and those emails flowed from George's fingers throughout the nights from the finance office of Sterling BMW. George had never really liked people face to face anyway, and he preferred his social contact to be virtual. Tracy was welcoming of George's interest.

And lest you think the bridge world a bunch of introverted math types, you are wrong. Players in the bridge community like to gossip and they like to be superior, especially the guy that invented the platform. Klaus Righteous once said to George, after George "blew the contract" during a game, "You stupid fool! One trick too early! The lead is in the dummy where your holding hearts K8!" He spoke as if he invented the game, and not just the IBA program.

One of the great players, according to Manny, was George's contact at IBA, Tracy Kettering, who was the tournament manager and also managed many national bridge events in England. Tracy was witty and a real master of ceremonies personality. You could see his charisma in the YouTube videos posted on the Club's website. He was a mathematician and musician who knew bridge and loved bridge people. George got up the nerve to ask Tracy for the IBA Java code and programming language. George explained he was a CPA quarantined in Newport Beach, California, and was passing the time with logic challenges. Tracy threw some code and numbers George's way, and that was all George needed to start his quiet but brilliant mind working on the site's problem.

After George got up to date on the IBA's code, he had 12 days left to figure out the glitch in the online automated gaming platform. If they never opened the quarantine doors, he would be happy if he could just convince the management at IBA they had a serious programming problem and to let him solve it for them. For the first time in his life, George had a personal goal. And he would achieve that goal. He would find the bug, and within a year he would reinvent the online bridge game. Singlehandedly, to pun a little.

Meanwhile, Manny played more and more boards of bridge and achieved remarkable feats of quick learning. A quality of his mechanical, logical, linear mind was that he could learn fast when he was learning about one topic. More than two topics in his head at once was too many. Quarantine, therefore, was the perfect place for Manny to conquer the game of bridge.

The white board on the wall in Sterling BMW's finance office was where Manny recorded his agonies and defeats, as well as his triumphs.

On the top of the white board, he had written: "The order of suits is clubs-diamonds-hearts-spades-no trump. Clubs being the lowest. When you bid 1-heart for example, you are saying you will take 6 of the 13 possible tricks (not necessarily heart tricks – just tricks during play). A bid of 3 hearts says you think you can take 9 of the 13 tricks. The only subsequent bid a player can make is higher. So, after a bid of 1-heart you cannot bid 1-club or 1-diamond."

He was a champion by nature, a competitive "type A" personality. He sought to conquer the International Bridge Association's best players in 15 days. So, whether or not he had mastered a problem, he made a note of his own progress, recorded also on the office white board:

I achieved a 21-point slam, 8-11-2020, 2 p.m.

I scored a 12-card fit, 8-13-2020, 11 a.m.

I got doubled and learned that strategy bid from the opposing team, 8-14-2020, 7:30 p.m.

I learned the optional double, 8-15-2020, 5:20 p.m.

I went for overtricks; I learned that every hand is played to first make the contract (bid) and I won't get penalized for taking more tricks than bid, so now I always try 8-16-2020, 10 a.m.
I achieved black suits to black horse, 8-20-2020, 8 p.m.
I got slammed, I learned to face it; the east west team just had a great hand, 8-25-2020, 4:30 p.m.
I scored a bottom, 8-26-2020, 9:45 p.m.
I learned the 30-point squeeze, 8-28-2020, 5 p.m.
I got the hang of grand bidding, 8-29-2020, 6:45 p.m.

His meticulous notes showed the single-minded concentration of a competitive, logical male.

George's contact in this new world of bridge, Tracy Kettering in London, suggested that George write an article on the probability of a player being dealt the same hand twice, and George had done the math and worked out the proofs. The article was called "Yes or No: Two Hands are Never the Same." George had submitted this article to the member players of IBA via their newsletter. This article sparked great acclaim for George but also controversy. Readers knew George had thought long and hard about this age-old question. George was making a name for himself for the first time in his life.

In the fall of 2020, after Mr. Sterling opened the door of the finance office and shook George and Manny's hands to say goodbye, the two formerly quarantined men remained friends and remained in the world of international bridge. It was lucky that the German engineer from BMW had upgraded George's computer when he did. Those 42 days with a superior computational device gave both men new careers and fresh starts in life.

Right around the time of their release, the founder of the International Bridge Association, Klaus Righteous, retired. So it's not surprising that George Smithson left

Sterling BMW (and the bossman Mr. Sterling) for good, and that Manny Nichols never returned to the engineering profession. Manny became an international bridge star and attended—and won—quite a few American Contract Bridge League tournaments in the spring, summer and fall. Manny won the McKenney Trophy, awarded to the top masterpoint player, chosen out of the top 500 individual players. By 2022, Manny would win the Masterpoint race.

The IBA offered George the director position, and he was handed the reins from founder Klaus Righteous after George's second article, "No Two Deals are Ever Alike," was published worldwide in *Scientific American*. The article was read with fervor by both the scientific and economic worlds, as it bordered on Game Theory, a hot topic. George, not quite a year after his lock-up in quarantine, lived a quiet but rewarding life in London, and he, in his own way, was a star in the bridge world as a master programmer. For a CPA who had never left the United States, London made George completely happy. He remained a US citizen, which was a fortuitous choice, because George became a MacArthur Fellow in 2021.

As director of the International Bridge Association's online automated gaming platform, George was head of software design and lead database programmer and researcher. His office was in the top floor garret of an 18th-century townhome in Kensington, which looked out on the great and historic city. George played a regular bridge game at the local pub with three other quiet ex-accountants. George's office at the International Bridge Association had a drawerful of Harrod's custom bowties. It also had its own loo, or, shall we say, W.C.

Chapter 15

Looking Out the Biggest Window

Eight-year-old Robert Ford Funicle, in lockdown with five adults, had a child's way of experiencing the quarantine. He was absorbing change without understanding the reasons for the change. The adults were speaking with each other about practical, actionable things, such as their work lives or the panicked global economy. Maturity often brings with it a certain level of intolerance for change, and strident complaints about the state of things often contain expectations based on the past.

But kids are different. Kids don't have much of a past. Children's worlds change every day, and coping with rapid change means that kids often enter a transition time, which creates a safe haven for their next step or next place. And so, in the conference room at Liederkranz, Campbell, Sheffield and Spray LLP, young Robert developed flexibility in a transition time. A child's ability to be flexible in the face of an emergency is perhaps a lesson for grown-ups. It will be Robert's generation that will face the integration of new realities, brought upon them by this new, uncharted world, which is not just a world of adult practicalities of careers, jobs, and money. The child feels something more.

Robert Funicle felt more alone in his lockdown than any of the adults. For most of his lockdown days, he stared out the corner window in the conference room and looked at the only piece of Washington, D.C., that he could see, a little pocket park with basketball hoops, tennis courts, and swing sets. And, like all children when faced with abrupt change, he first felt sorry for himself. Then he thought of other people, and again looked outside at the park below, and he thought of the world. How were other people doing? Did they look sad? Where were all the kids? What were they doing for fun? Did they feel scared? None of the self-centered adults in the conference room was doing that kind of thinking or looking.

Dr. and Mrs. Funicle were in the kitchenette of the conference room at Liederkranz, Campbell, Sheffield and Spray LLP. Mrs. Mary Funicle was re-preparing a tuna casserole that had been delivered through the small window by the State.

She thought of her mother, who grew up during the Depression. "Leonard, Momma would have saved half this casserole, you know. She never recovered from the 1930s when the family had very little, and insecurity was a daily fact. She saved string, she saved Green Stamps, she saved old worn socks. To save these things gave her a sense of control over her entire life. You remember Momma, dear?"

That wonderful, stalwart generation that had faced insecurity as children during the Great Depression would never forget the lessons of austerity and caution. Reedley, when he overheard Mrs. Funicle's comment, thought about Amalie's son, Robert, and he thought about how Robert would deal with the pandemic's lessons of fear and insecurity in his future.

The last half of the 42 days of lockdown found the inhabitants of the conference room in different corners. In one corner, Amalie and Carol read law books. They made marginal notes in pencil, laughed about the ironies in the law regarding ethics and punishment, and prepared an application for law school.

In the kitchen, Dr. and Mrs. Funicle, who were disappointed by the State's catered food, worked on each meal. They improved each dish with the meager supplies found in Carol's office larder.

In the corner of the conference room with the side window that overlooked the pocket park, Reedley and young Robert Funicle had set up a folding table on which Reedley had repurposed an old IBM Selectric typewriter for Robert. He had coached him on learning to type, and the noise of his little fingers was pleasant to hear. On a late day in quarantine, Robert and Reedley had been hunkered over this antique tool together, one small head with its beautiful mane of flowing red hair, and one oddly shaped, slightly balding head, with a suggestion of comb-over, joining. Together they peered deep into the 40-year-old platen.

Robert had been withdrawn, but the grown-up people didn't understand why. The pandemic had severed the inter-generational relationships Robert enjoyed. On his mom's farm, he had seven moms and their friends and families to guide him and play with him. Many different people used to joke with him and tell him what to do, and he loved gathering the chicken eggs every day. He missed seeing the oldest mother, who was 40, because she was the fattest and her lap was the warmest when she read him poetry.

Crisis and disaster are not new, but the traditional ways generations have banded together to stay safe and sane were as distant for Robert as the social distancing rules he would face for years. Although there were three generations in the conference room, the grown-ups did not talk to him about the strange things that were happening. The masks Robert could see from the window on the faces of pedestrians might have been superhero masks, but Robert would learn soon enough those masks symbolized powerlessness, not power.

Robert was aware of a big change, but because he was eight, he didn't completely understand how these changes would change him. Later in life, he would realize that he had spent some of his childhood in quarantine coping with a once-in-a-generation shift. The lingering effects on a child his age were yet to be seen, but he was trying to understand his new world—perhaps more profoundly than the adults around him.

The adults were attempting to get through their days. But Robert was looking out on the big world outside that window in the corner. Sometimes he tried to get the adults interested in something outside of that room. "Look, Grandma, I see a stray dog! Where's his home?" he'd say, or "Mom, come here! I think I see another kid!" Once he said, "Look at that park, Reedley. I hope I see someone playing there soon." Robert, receiving only single word answers from the grown-ups began to write little short lines on the IBM Selectric, telling the typewriter what he had seen out that corner window.

ELIZABETH STEWART

Robert had a secret weapon that some children have: a unique and instinctive sensitivity. He could actively put himself in the place of others. Someday that sensitivity would make him a great actor; it would let the universe into his heart, and he would laugh and cry deeply in equal measure. His journey of empathy, and his path as an artist, began in that conference room.

Reedley had grown fond of Robert and had seen the depth of heart in the child. Reedley began to reflect upon his previous fantasy around Robert's mother, Amalie. He grew ashamed of himself for having lost that bigness of heart he saw in Robert. He was trying to recover from adult selfishness, and when Robert couldn't find kids in the park below, Reedley had listened to Robert's concerns about other children.

Robert told Reedley that children made up almost half of the world, so where were they playing now? Reedley, a mature, middle-aged man, was humbled by that little child. Reedley, too, looked through the big window into the long streets below, but the gray rain was falling on only adult heads, bent under the weight of getting through the day.

Robert was silently concerned for everybody. Reedley saw in Robert's gaze that his love for the world was an active expression that looked outside of himself. Reedley felt close to the little boy, seeing himself at that age. Reedley rediscovered that love happens across generations and genders, and had very little to do with a person's exterior make and model.

Reedley had believed, during the first days of the lockdown, that Robert would feel the effects of quarantine less than the adults. No one worried about Robert. But early on, Robert seemed to retreat into his own space, and began to gaze out the window for hours, looking for other children. The adults talked themselves out of worrying about little Robert.

"Robert is a child! He will bounce back. Children are resilient!" the adults said. Robert listened to the grown-ups as he looked out the window, and what he heard

171

made him think adults didn't know much about children his age.

Sure, they gave Robert activities so he wouldn't be bored, but Robert was somehow disappointed in the adults. They seemed to think only of themselves, and only of surviving the next few weeks. Reedley was the only one who he could talk to. Robert told Reedley, "I feel like I am 'in between' now. I am in between happy and sad, real life and make-believe, and in between my old place and my new one. Why do you think that is?" Reedley had no answer; he remained silent and reflexive.

Indeed, Reedley thought, what about the kids? Who was thinking of the kids? Children like Robert might be emotionally affected by the quarantine, and affected during a much longer lifespan. Children may adapt, but for a while they may remain in a unique liminal space.

"Will I always feel alone in a roomful of people?" Robert asked no one, just the window. That was the big question. The child asked it of himself.

Robert, in a few short years, would take that feeling of obscure but perceptible discontent into his adult life. What he had experienced in the days of quarantine, his sense of being "in between" a present reality and the world of imagination, would fuel his growth as a creative artist.

As Robert plunked out his words on the IBM Selectric one windy afternoon, Reedley asked, "Robert, what do you think about when you look out of the window?"

"Well, Mr. Liederkranz, I think about the world, and the world makes me think about what I feel inside me." Reedley was stuck by this simple phrase. Robert looked up at Reedley from his composition at the typewriter and continued, pointing to a leaf in the wind. "I feel like that leaf. I am here, but I am out there too. I am connected to both the inside and the outside. I can imagine that I am in both places at once. And it makes me happy, because I am connected to both places."

Grace is possible when a person is invited, or even forced, to rethink his life.

Reedley was doing just that, because of Robert. Had Reedley been so small as to believe that his goal of connectivity was to be found with a make-believe woman, selfishly designed for his eyes only?

No, Reedley thought. To love someone else, you have to go outside of yourself. He had lost sight of that in his marriage and in his vocation. Why? he asked himself. He whispered to himself, "I was afraid."

He thought of the little boy, and wondered if Robert was hiding his fear. Robert must be given a way to express himself—and then, be heard, and be taken seriously! Fear brews inside young ones, and can be lessened through invention and creativity, with a little space to make a connection to imagination, thought Reedley. When we invent something, we control our experience.

Robert looked away from his typewriter and tried to listen to the growing buzz of adult conversation in the conference room. The adults were talking about tactics to get them through their days, preoccupied with getting past the quarantine. They talked of serious things like money, mortgages, banks, jobs. Robert listened to Carol and his mother as they chattered about the law. He listened to his grandfather and grandmother talk about food, money, and survival techniques. Robert did not think he would be taken seriously at all if he suggested a game of hide-and-seek or a poem. He didn't think their grown-up attitude was going to change much if he suggested a race across the conference room. He began to run around the room on his own.

At the point of a near collision, Robert's grandmother gently stopped the little boy. "Where are you off to, little lad?" she said, leaning to his level.

"When do you think that life will be fun again, Grandma?" His grandmother had no answer for the boy. Maybe that was because she was too old to remember what fun felt like.

"Just get me through this day," his grandmother said in reply. So Robert amused himself by listened to the crows outside the window rasp away; they didn't care about the adult world inside.

Robert wondered what was going to happen after this was over. Life was bigger than 42 days. Even though 42 days is a lifetime for an eight-year-old used to sunshine and chickens and laughter, he was wise beyond his years. Robert had the sense that if they all tried, they could think beyond the moment and not feel so constricted. I wish the adults would look outside the window, he thought. The world is big!

Unlike any other person in the law firm's conference room, Robert felt empathy for the world outside, although he didn't know the word for it.

Reedley was moved. He saw the concern on Robert's face. He longed for a passageway, a vehicle, a vessel, an avenue for Robert to create and express himself. It became obvious to him as he watched Robert gaze out of the window that he had to do something. Robert needed to do what the adults had taught themselves not to do: to play, pretend, reflect, and dream, and get beyond the strictures of time. What could Reedley give Robert?

He remembered his theological school training and the Bible verse Matthew 19:14, the "Suffer the little children" passage. It says that those who enter the Kingdom of God must do so as a little child. That verse spoke to Reedley about the hope of trust in life, and the promise of joy in the big wide world. Would this generation of children have a reason to trust life? They might, thought Reedley, if we teach them how to embrace their innate creativity.

For the first time in 20 years, Reedley prayed. "God, help me to find a way to empower this young child. Help me to help him find his voice." In this prayer, Reedley was asking what many people might ask: How may I help others express what makes them whole?

Reedley concocted a plan to teach Robert about the life of words. He read to Robert from children's poetry books from the extensive law library. One of the poems brought Reedley back to his childhood and made Reedley cry like a baby.

"Don't cry, Mr. Liederkranz," Robert said. "I think you're crying because you don't like that poem. But I can write you one you will like better that won't make you cry!" Robert sat down at the IBM Selectric on the folding table in the corner, and began to compose a poem. Reedley then discovered Robert's gift, which was the innocent and pure love of the written word, conveyed with imagination.

Reedley, when he read Robert's poem, had an inspiration. He reached out to his old parish, where he had formerly led the Methodist Church of Arlington, and, after begging their forgiveness, he established a daily newsletter called "Poems from an 8-Year-Old," a fundraising platform for Arlington Methodist's sister church in Mombasa called the Mombasa Crisis Resilience Fund. The fund aimed to help children under 12 in families with no access to healthcare, in anticipation of the second wave of the pandemic. Robert composed twelve poems for twelve editions of the newsletter.

Writing poems together was like child's play for both Robert and Reedley. At the end of the quarantine, Reedley was a softer man, because he had risked caring for someone other than himself. This is what children teach us if we are wise enough to be taught. We can take a chance in love and friendship because we can trust in life. We can connect with others and, with imagination, forget ourselves. Reedley and little red-headed Robert leaned over the IBM Selectric and read Robert's final poem together.

"Looking out of the Big Window"

The hoops in our park across the street are boarded up, and that park is lonely.
The grass below the hoops wants to see and feel children's feet.
The grass wants to feel a grandmother's shoes, and a mother's stroller.
Beyond the park, I can see the Big City with no people, and I hear the City with no voice.

I can hear loud sandpaper birds, the black crows: too many black crows.
The biggest crow perches on the saddest hoop above the grass.
The only sound the City makes is an ambulance wail, and it makes the dogs cry.

Yesterday I saw three kids, and the park smiled because they had come.
The park loved the feeling of the drawings they made with chalk on the three big tennis courts.
The kids came for three days. They drew, and then they went home.
They made colored chalk patterns that went round and round, like a maze.

The round swirls of their designs came off on their clothes.

Maybe they are Saints, like the Bible Saints we read about, because they are drawing a message for the future, and because they have appeared from nowhere.
Maybe they are small Saint Children, making chalk marks so big that adults now have a direction to follow, even though a maze has no direction.

Written on their chalk hands and knees, they bring a colorful message home to their families.

Reedley felt tears in his eyes. The poem was simple and evocative, a perfect goodbye to the lockdown, and a somber hello to the future.

"And what was the message, Robert, that the children brought home?" asked Reedley.

Robert said, "Mr. Liederkranz! Don't you know? That message is hope!"

And then Reedley and Robert joined hands and raced around the conference room at Liederkranz, Campbell, Sheffield and Spray LLP.

Elizabeth and her companions John
and Bear, Quarantine, Spring 2020

About the Author

Elizabeth Stewart is an arts journalist, a professional certified appraiser of art, and a storyteller. She was educated at Tufts University, Edinburgh University, and USD, and she holds a PhD in Myth and Psychology from Pacifica Graduate Institute. This is her fourth book; other titles include *Collect Value Divest: The Savvy Appraiser, No Thanks Mom: The Top Ten Things Your Kids Do Not Want,* and *The Ten Worst Things Not to Do in a Disaster.*

www.ingramcontent.com/pod-product-compliance
Lightning Source LLC
Chambersburg PA
CBHW041157100726
47911CB00016B/774